Brou~~ght to~~

The Wilkester Mysteries (Book 1)

BROUGHT
TO BOOK

BARBARA CORNTHWAITE

the wilkester mysteries book one

The Wilkester Mysteries (Book 1)

ISBN: 9798657044126

Edited by: Coyle Editing Services
Fonts: Garamond,
Cover art by: Joshua Markey

Connect with Me Online:
My newsletter
Amazon Author Page: https://www.amazon.com/Barbara-Cornthwaite/e/B00J47TTZM
BookBub:
Facebook: https://www.facebook.com/barbara.cornthwaite
Goodreads:
https://www.goodreads.com/author/show/3256827.Barbara_Cornthwaite
Website: https://barbaracornthwaite.com

The events and people in this book, aside from the caveats on the next page, are purely fictional, and any resemblance to actual people is purely coincidental and I'd love to meet them!

CHAPTER 1

Frank's Book Store had an antique little bell that tinkled when the front door was opened. It was an old-world place that would have been right at home on a side street in Oxford, or better yet, Hay-on-Wye. As it was, it stood in the center of a mid-sized town in Washington State, flanked by Save-U-Bucks Discount Market on one side and a cell phone store on the other. To be sure, the back of the property shared a boundary with Wilkester College, which seemed appropriate, and a little alleyway connected it to that institution of higher learning. If the path had come anywhere near the English department it would have been ideal. However, it was the Mathematics department that was nearest to the bookstore, and although there are those who see poetry and even music in numbers, all they have ever represented to me is torture and despair.

Frank himself seemed a little out of place in his own store. Some of his qualities were what you might imagine in a dealer in old books: he was an elderly little man who eschewed modern technology to such an extent that he owned no cell phone and used an ancient computer grudgingly and only for email—finally being convinced that for the sake of his business he needed to communicate with customers and suppliers in a method other than paper letters sent through the post office.

On the other hand, he was not so delightful a

gentleman as you might think. When I first encountered him in his store I expected him to know a great deal about the world of literature, to be in love with the feel and the smell of old books, and to rejoice in a first edition of, for example, *Humphry Clinker*. I thought he ought to have a twinkle in his eye, a pixie-like sense of humor, and a fount of ready wit, which he used when bantering with customers. Alas, he was a curmudgeon of the first order with no poetry at all in his soul. You could guess that, couldn't you, from the name of his business? With all the witty and charming possibilities for the name of a place that sold old books, he chose to name it Frank's Book Store.

He was not one of the world's great organizers, nor did he specialize in any particular kind of book. He bought any volume that had covers with words in between and he shelved them all alphabetically by title, so that a racy romance novel like *Nights of Passion* was right next to a scholarly work like *Nigerian Statesmen 1960-1985*.

One day after a particularly frustrating morning of teaching the twenty-three students who attended my American Lit class at the college—apparently for no better reason than being read to sleep—I could not tolerate the odd juxtapositions any longer.

"Look," I said, irritation overcoming my natural deference, "do you mind if I move some of the more valuable old books to that empty set of shelves over there?"

"Then they won't all be alphabetical," Frank said.

"I'll arrange those shelves alphabetically *by author*, and when someone asks if you have a book by Edgar Allan Poe, you'll be able to find it quickly. As it is, you can only find books in your store if you know the titles. You're probably losing money as a result."

His mouth twitched as he thought it over. "You think I'll make more money that way?"

"Absolutely."

"How long will it take you? I don't want you to start the job and then disappear and leave it all a mess." He fixed me with a grim stare. I started to feel like I was ten instead of nearly forty-two.

"I can come in for a couple hours every day until it's done," I said. "I'm here almost that often anyway. And I can probably finish in a week."

There was another silence.

"Well, all right." He sighed as if he had made a supreme sacrifice, and went back to his little desk on which the telephone, a mammoth old desktop computer, and a pile of invoices reposed, leaving only enough room for a mug of coffee and the ledger he was trying to balance.

It was one of the most enjoyable weeks I had had in years, finding the treasures amid all the twaddle and the negligible books. When I was finished, I pointed out to Frank which books were worth good money and suggested he either advertise them or send them to auction. He did so and made a tidy profit.

After that it was easy for me to suggest that I should be allowed to organize the rest of the books into groups— at first merely nonfiction and fiction, and then as the months went by into more sophisticated categories.

As time went on, Frank appeared to forget I was not an employee. Whenever new books came in he'd tell me that I needed to get them shelved, and when someone emailed him to ask if he had any books that were published before 1730, he put the question to me. Eventually, of course, my time filled up with other activities—I did some freelance editing, I started a book club at the library, I began teaching a Sunday School class, I made a few more friends—and my time at the bookstore dwindled to a mere couple of hours a week. I wouldn't say that Frank was overjoyed to see me when I came in, but he did say, "Oh, there you are!" as if he had been waiting for me.

He said it with more emphasis than usual on a freezing cold March afternoon when I slipped in after my English Composition class. "I have a question to ask you," he added.

"Katrina to the rescue," I murmured.

"How hard is it to forge something? Like a literary thing."

I raised my eyebrows. "Thinking of starting a second business?"

"No, no, no," he snapped. "Just answer the question."

"Well, it depends on a lot of things. How old is the manuscript? Is it handwritten or printed? Is it a whole book or just one sheet of paper?"

"Let's say something handwritten that's a couple hundred years old."

"In that case, you would need to find paper manufactured in that era, since paper is made differently now. You'd also need ink that was right for the period, and a pen—probably a quill pen that was also from the right era. You'd also need to be able to fake the handwriting of the period, which is hard to do, and if there is already a known sample of the author's handwriting, you'd have to copy it perfectly. And if you're making up something for the person to have written, you'd better know the spelling, punctuation, vocabulary, and syntax of the time. It's not something an amateur could whip up in their spare time and fool people."

"Hm. I see." He turned back to his desk.

"Do you think you might have accidentally bought a forgery?"

"No," he answered shortly.

Well, that was that.

I wandered back to my new favorite section: Historical nonfiction. I found the book I had discovered last week: an etiquette handbook from the 1940's. Dear Emily Post had the answer for every kind of social question: how to politely word refusals of marriage, which kind of thank you note should be sent in which circumstance, what kind of and how many clothes a college student should take with them to school, and what sort of uniform your maid should wear. I smiled at the confident assertion that "a lady never leaves the house without her hat and gloves."

The telephone rang—a jarring sound in this age of muted electronic chimes and beeps. I could hear Frank's grunted "hello." There was silence as I turned the page to find out in what circumstance a veil might properly be worn with a hat.

"I told you no before, and I'll say it again," said Frank. "It's no good you calling me and asking me over and over. That's final." There was more of an edge to his voice than usual.

"That's a threat," he went on after a moment, "An empty threat. And you don't frighten me." The phone clunked as Frank hung up, and I could hear him muttering to himself. I came out from behind the back shelves with my finger still in the book.

"What's wrong?" I asked.

"It's that college of yours. Wants me to sell the building to them. Again."

I nodded. "Yes, I heard about that. They want to use it as the college bookstore. They're thinking of turning the current one into a fast food place."

"Well you can tell them from me that they can just give up trying. I'm not selling. You tell those people that."

"They won't listen to me," I said. "I'm only an adjunct faculty member. No clout at all."

"I'm not selling."

"All right then," I said. "What was that about a threat?"

"Nothing." He turned abruptly back to his work and I went back to Emily Post. I wanted to find out how to dress my nanny. In case, you know, I should ever have one and she should want to dress like someone living in 1945.

"By the way," Frank said, "There's a shipment of books coming in tomorrow for you to shelve. Got them from the Wilkes estate."

"*The* Wilkes estate? The family of the man there's a statue of in front of City Hall?"

"Yep. Old fellow finally died—about ninety-five years old. He's some descendant of the statue man."

"He was the man who founded Wilkester, wasn't he? In 1855 or so?"

"Right."

"That's what I thought. I have one of his descendants in my writing class. He wrote a paper about it."

Frank snorted. "I'll bet he did. Those Wilkeses think they're the royalty of Pierce County. They get all kinds of special treatment for being old Matthew Wilkes's family— college scholarships, opening festivals, leading the Fourth of July parade, being written up in the newspaper whenever they do something…"

"Matt certainly is proud of his family," I said charitably. "His paper mentioned that the first Matthew Wilkes saved a bunch of people in a flood, or something, as the town was being founded."

Frank rolled his eyes. "When I was a child in elementary school, there was a pageant every year re-enacting that event. We're all sick of that story around here."

There didn't seem to be any point in prolonging the conversation. Frank picked up his pencil again, and I returned to Emily Post. In case you were wondering, a nanny should be dressed in the cap and cape of a British nanny *only* if she herself is British.

The Coles invited me over for dinner that night. It's amazing how restful it is to be with them, in spite of their crazy household: two parents, three teenagers, two elementary-aged foster kids, and an assortment of pets. Ed and Kim have known me long enough that I'm not self-conscious around them, which is a lovely thing. I hadn't realized, before I moved, how nerve-wracking it is to go to a place where you know practically no one. Every time you meet a new person you're making a first impression that you will either have to live up to or try to live down. And when you see those people for the second time you're trying to remember if you made a good or bad impression on them and wondering what you should be doing to reinforce whatever good they saw and invalidate the bad. And of course it's stressful and ridiculous to live that way (not to mention the whole fear-of-man thing the Bible is so vocal about), so I determined early on that I would just be myself without any regard for what people thought of me. And thereafter I had to ask myself every five minutes, "Am I being myself? Would I have said that or done that if I were being myself?" And I can never quite be sure.

Maybe it's just me.

Anyway, I met Ed and Kim in college—we were part of the same campus Bible study. They moved up here soon after we graduated, but we kept in touch. In fact, it was Ed's idea for me to apply for the job here in Wilkester—he's the Vice President for Academic Affairs at the college.

Dinner was a little chaotic, as the newest child they're fostering, aged seven, threw his plate against the wall and ran out the front door in the middle of the meal. I suppose it might have shocked me once, but in the last couple of years I've seen them care for several foster kids with trauma issues and throwing a plate of food against the wall ranks as a fairly mild interruption. Both parents mobilized to get him back inside, but the rest of us continued eating. Once little Ben was back in the house, Kim stayed with him in his room to help him calm down, and Ed came back to the table and finished his meal.

"That didn't take too long," I commented.

"No, he's getting better. In fact, he kept looking behind him to make sure we were following him. Kim might be down before long."

Actually, she didn't come down for another half-hour. By that time we had finished eating and I had volunteered to start the dishes so the teens could finish their homework and Ed could spend a little time with Mia, the five-year-old. Kim joined me in cleaning up the kitchen.

"All serene?"

"Yeah, he's fine now. I'll read him his story before bed, but he's working at his homework now."

"There's such a huge change in him from a few months ago when he first came. Remember that tantrum that lasted twelve hours?"

Kim nodded. "That was the worst. Sometimes it seems like it's been so bad for so long, but then I look back and see just how much improvement there has been."

"You guys are doing so much good."

She looked at me slyly. "You could too…they're really short of foster parents right now."

I laughed. "Can you see me as a foster parent?"

Kim finished drying the pot she was holding and put it away. "I can, actually. You'd be great."

"You know I'd love to, but I work! Not only that, but I work a weird schedule! I only have a two-bedroom apartment!"

"None of those things are really barriers, you know. And you love kids. You're good with kids. You like making a difference. I could help you."

I kept wiping the counter. There was something in the idea that attracted me.

"At least think about it," said Kim.

"All right, I'll add it to the list."

"List of what?"

"Things I'm thinking about." I threw away the paper towel I'd been using and found the broom.

"Like?"

"You know the mission school Carrie teaches at in Papua New Guinea? They're looking for teachers next year." Carrie was another old friend from our college Bible study.

"Wow." Kim stopped moving to absorb that idea. "Is that something you'd like to do?"

"Like I said, I'm thinking about it." I kept sweeping. "My career isn't really going the way I thought it would. After what happened at UCSC, and then only getting this adjunct professor work afterwards… The chances of me being hired as full-time faculty are very, very slim. You know that adjunct faculty members aren't paid much—if it weren't for the money from editing I couldn't make it. I don't really want to spend the rest of my life doing this." I found the dustpan and began to sweep the debris into it. "I used to think of my teaching as something I could do until I got married. But marriage looks more unlikely every year."

I can only say that to a few chosen souls. Most people feel impelled to respond with, "Oh, don't give up hope! My aunt didn't get married until she was forty-nine!" and I really don't need to hear that. Kim, bless her, never said it to me.

All she said now was, "What do your parents think? And your brother?"

"I haven't told them. I already know what they'll say: 'You have a Ph.D.. Surely you don't mean to waste it on some elementary-aged kids!' I can see their point, but I feel like I could be of more use to the Lord doing that than what I'm doing now. I am single. I can pick up and move across the world if I want to. Most people can't."

"You could be used by God in foster care, too."

"True. Like I said, I'll add it to the things I'm thinking about."

Kim sighed. "I wouldn't want to see you go across the world, but that's selfish. I'll pray with you about it."

"Thanks." I put back the dustpan and broom and gave her a hug. "You're the best."

CHAPTER 2

The weather had warmed up a little bit by the time I went back to the bookstore a few days later. The bell tinkled cheerfully as I opened the door. I remember that because it was the last time I ever heard that sound with pleasure.

"Katrina, you're back," said Frank.

"In the flesh," I agreed. "Anything new?"

"You missed the scene yesterday." He grimaced, which is as close as Frank ever got to a smile. "Didn't you say you had one of the Wilkes kids in your class?"

"Yes, Matt. He likes old books and I told him he'd enjoy your store. Did he come in?"

Frank chuckled dryly. "He did. He said he wanted to see my old books, and I pointed out the shelves in the back where you put them, and he went back to look at them. And guess what else is on those shelves?"

"I don't know. There wasn't anything else there last week."

"Remember I told you I bought a bunch of books from the Wilkes estate? Well, I had to put them somewhere, so I stuck them there on the empty shelves near the bottom until you would come in and put them in the right places. You haven't been here in a few days."

"Sorry," I murmured, just as though I deserved some

reproach. It was a reflex.

"As I said, he was looking at those shelves and he saw some of the books from the estate. And he found this one." Frank picked up a book from his desk and handed it to me.

"Very old," I said. "Handwritten. A day-book or journal of some kind." I turned to the flyleaf at the front of it and found a name: Matthew Wilkes. I looked at the dates—it appeared to start in 1848.

"Do you think…?" I asked. "The town's founder?"

"Not only do I think it, but your student thought so, too. First he told me that I had no right to the book and that it ought to stay in the family. 'I'm a Wilkes,' he said, 'and you need to listen to me!' Little punk thinks his word is law. Well, not in my store. I told him I bought it from the estate and it was all perfectly legal for me to have it. Then he said he wanted to buy it. And I told him"—Frank paused to let an expression of pure gloating flicker over his face—"I told him it ought to go to a museum here in town because it was a historical document. And that I wouldn't sell it to him."

He was clearly proud of himself for finding a way to frustrate someone from the hated family of Wilkes.

"Hmmm," I said. "You may be right about the museum, but I think this might be something for a lawyer to determine."

Frank made a sound like "Bah!" and at that moment he looked every bit as misanthropic as a Dickensian villain. "That kid said, 'I'll get it back. You'll see.' Like a threat."

"You might want to put it away safely somewhere— just in case he's tempted to steal it."

"Oh, I will. Maybe I'll get a safe."

"A safe would be a good idea," I said. "And if you were ever going to expand this place, or have more rare books, you could have a locked cabinet for them."

"Is that what they have at that college of yours? They have old books, but I thought anyone could just go in and look at them."

"You mean the manuscripts and first editions that were willed to the college by some benefactor?"

"Right. They used to be in the library. I saw them a bunch of times."

I raised my eyebrows. Frank had such disdain for the college and so little reverence for anything literary that it was hard to imagine him frequently going to stare at these items.

"Why?"

For a moment I thought he wasn't going to answer. Then he said gruffly, "Someone I used to know was interested in them." His mouth clamped shut after that and I knew it was the only explanation I was going to get.

"Well, they might have been out in the open back then," I said, "But for a long time they've been in a locked room in the back of the library that you need special permission to access."

"Have you seen them?"

"Yes. I got the teaching job there partly because my dissertation was on Anne Bradstreet's poetry, and the college has the only manuscript in existence of one of her poems. It's a fair copy—one that is finished and ready to send to a printer."

"It's valuable, then?"

"Extremely. It wasn't even brought to light until about twenty-five years ago. I was a college freshman then, and I remember how exciting it was that such a thing existed. In fact," I went on, "I think that's why I developed such an interest in her poetry."

He appeared to lose interest in the conversation when I launched into my personal biography, because he

17

turned and went into the little closet where the cleaning supplies and the odds-and-ends of the store collected, still clutching the journal of Matthew Wilkes. I supposed he was going to try to hide it in there. I went back to the shelves where Frank had put the new books from the Wilkes estate and started looking through them to see where they ought to be shelved.

Many of them had not been opened for years and years—possibly a hundred or more. There were a couple of handwritten volumes: not only the journal of Matthew Wilkes, but an account book from the late Victorian age tracking the household expenses. That would be a treasure for a historian that studied this region; what things were bought and how much they cost at a certain time and place is something historians are always trying to find out.

There was also the usual quota of deeply moral and badly-written stories that parents and teachers used to give children in the nineteenth century. I paused to caress the cover of one of them—the outside, of it, at least, was a beautiful thing. The soft green was embossed with gold letters that read *Boys of Valor*, and it was the perfect size to fit into a deep pocket. The next book was a handsomely bound copy of *Timothy's Quest* by Kate Douglas Wiggin. I checked the date of printing—1894, twelfth edition, in London. And it included a prefatory note from the author explaining how pleased she was about the wide acceptance of her work in England. That was interesting—someone in the Wilkes family must have travelled to England at some point and picked up this book. Perhaps they wanted an American tale to entertain them while they were abroad?

I sat on the floor and opened it. It had been years since I had read this. "Minerva Court! Veil thy face, O Goddess of Wisdom, for never, surely, was thy fair name so ill bestowed as when it was applied to this most dreary place."

The bell over the door of the store tinkled as someone came in. Grateful that I couldn't be seen, I hoped Frank would be able to handle the customer on his own and not interrupt my reading. I could hear Frank get up from the desk and move toward the front of the store.

"Are you Frank?" said a man's voice.

"Yep."

There was silence for a moment and then there was a bang. A very loud bang. I jumped and then froze. *That was a gunshot.* There was a sound like someone falling down. *Stay still. Stay still. Don't move. Don't move.* The thoughts repeated themselves over and over. I tried to breathe silently, but my heart was pounding so hard I was sure I could hear it outside my body—and so could anyone else. *Please, God, keep me safe. Don't let the man look around the store. Please make him leave.*

It took about a minute, I think, maybe less. I heard the bell tinkle again. *He's gone.* Still I didn't move. *What if he comes back? What if he's waiting to see if someone comes out of the store? What if he's still in here and trying to make me think he's gone?*

I sat there for another minute. *What if Frank needs my help? Dear Lord, what if Frank needs help?*

I had to see if I could help. If I died, at least I would die trying to do the right thing. Cautiously I put down *Timothy's Quest* and crept down the aisle between the shelves and then past the other four rows of shelves out into the open part of the store. Frank was there, face down, on the ground. There was a puddle of blood under him.

"Frank?" I whispered. There was no response. I crawled over to him and tried to feel for a pulse. I'm one of those people that has a hard time finding my own pulse, let alone someone else's. I couldn't feel anything. That might have been because my heart was still pounding and I was shaking so badly I could hardly pull my phone out of my pocket.

9-1-1.

"911, What's your emergency?" It was a female voice.

"Someone's been shot," I whispered. "I don't know if the man with the gun will come back. I don't want to talk much."

"Where are you?"

"Frank's Book Store on Elvery Avenue in Wilkester."

"Is there somewhere you can go to be safe?"

"I think so."

"Go there and stay on the line. I have help on the way. Stay on the line if you can, but you don't need to talk."

I got up from where I was crouching beside Frank and ran to the closet. I pulled the door shut behind me and found there was a lock on it. I locked it.

"I'm in the closet in the back," I whispered into the phone.

"All right," said the voice. "Just stay there until the police arrive."

I sat quietly in the dark with only the faint light from my phone shining up from the floor where I had laid it. *Please, God, let Frank be all right. He doesn't know You. I shared the gospel with him once…please let him be ok.* Time passed slowly in the silent dark. I was conscious of every single breath. After several minutes had gone by, I could hear sirens. They were very faint at first but grew louder with every second.

"Wilkester Police!" shouted a voice as the little bell tinkled and there were footsteps—more than belonged to just one person.

"I'm in the closet!" I called. "I'm the one who called 911!"

"Stay there, ma'am, for just a minute." I could picture the policemen roaming around the store with their weapons out, the way they do in detective shows.

"It's safe to come out now," said a voice. "But come out slowly with your hands where we can see them."

Of course, I thought. *They don't know if I'm the shooter or not.* I stood up and slowly opened the door with one hand while the other was up in the air. There were two policemen right in front of me. They only had their guns trained on me for a second. Then I saw them relax.

"It's over," one of them told me. And to my horror and great embarrassment, I burst into tears.

CHAPTER 3

I sat at a table in a small, windowless room at the police station with a bottle of water someone had given me and a box of tissues the police officer had handed to me when she put me in the room. I had sniveled my way through the process of being fingerprinted and having my details taken down. The fact that I was still crying an hour after I emerged from the closet was fairly humiliating. I had the sensation of being "handled"—not that the officers were unsympathetic or rude, but they must have seen weak, shaken women dozens of times and weren't unduly stirred by my emotion. I wanted Kim or someone who could say, "How terrible! I can't imagine what you're going through!" and give me a hug.

A detective would be coming to talk to me, I was told. I tried to calm myself down. The odd thing was, I wasn't really all that mentally disturbed. It had been a shock, of course, but God had protected me. Frank was dead—I knew that before I had been whisked out of the bookstore—and there was nothing I could have done about that. As far as I knew, he had died without Christ. That was the worst part. I also knew that nothing I could have done would have made him believe the gospel I had told him; my duty had been to tell him, and the rest I could leave with God. I couldn't understand why I was still crying. That is, I could make myself stop and be calm for a while, but a few minutes later the tears would come again.

The door opened and a man came in. He looked official but was wearing a suit instead of a uniform. He sat down across from me at the table.

"Hello, Ms. Peters. I'm Detective Todd Mason. I need to ask you some questions, if that's all right."

"Miss," I said without thinking. I hate Ms.

"I beg your pardon?"

"It's *Miss* Peters," I said, and then blushed. Why would I make a big deal about it at a time like this? Making sure he knew I was single! He must think I was some kind of man-hunting floozy. I looked at his ring finger involuntarily—he had no wedding ring. "Never mind," I added in a small voice.

I thought he smiled faintly. He looked like a nice person—about my age, with brown hair and brown eyes that looked tired. I would have liked to make a better first impression.

"Miss Peters," he corrected himself. "Can you tell me why you were at the bookstore? Did you come in to buy something?"

"Not exactly. I was working. Sort of. I guess you could call me a volunteer."

"You volunteer at a bookstore? Like a charity?"

"No, not really a charity. I used to go in there a lot to read the books and then I started helping out..."

"I see. So you knew the victim well."

I nodded. More tears were falling and I grabbed a tissue.

"Do you have a job besides volunteering at the bookstore?"

"Yes, I teach at Wilkester College and do some freelance editing."

He wrote all that down.

"Were you there volunteering today?"

"Yes. I was organizing some books on the shelves near the back. I showed the policemen where I was when they came to the bookstore."

"So you couldn't really see what happened."

"No. I just heard things."

"Can you tell me exactly what you heard, please?"

"I heard the door open—at least, I heard the bell ring and the noise of traffic on the street got louder, and I knew someone had come in. And then I heard Frank get up from his desk—he always grunted a little when he got up—and go out toward the open area. The man said, 'Are you Frank?' and Frank said yes."

"Did you recognize the voice?"

"No. I mean, it was only three words, and the voice was quiet. It wasn't someone I know well, I'm sure of that." I paused, trying to think if I had heard anything else before the fatal moment. I couldn't remember anything. "Then there was a bang. Really loud. I don't know why I didn't scream—I usually scream when I'm surprised."

"It might have saved your life that you kept quiet."

"Must have been God closing my mouth, like the lions," I said, more to myself than anything. I saw Detective Mason's eyebrows go up and that faint smile came again.

"And then," I said hurriedly, "I heard a thump like someone falling—I'm sure it was Frank falling down."

"Did either of them say anything else?"

"No, nothing. I remember some faint noises like maybe the man was moving around. I was just so scared he was going to search the store or something and find me."

"And how long did that go on?"

I wiped another tear that had come trickling down my face. "I'm sorry," I put in. "I don't know why I'm still crying." I took a deep breath. "I don't think it went on for very long. Maybe a minute? It felt like forever. I never thought about looking at my watch or anything."

"No one would expect you to," he said as he wrote down my answer. "And don't worry about the tears. It's just a physical response to shock. You're doing very well." His eyes met mine. It was the first moment of real comfort I had had since the shooting.

"What happened after that?"

"I heard the bell ring and the door open, so I thought he must have left. I wasn't sure, though—I thought maybe he might come back in or maybe he had pretended to leave to see if anyone would come out, so I just stayed there for a while. Probably another minute or two."

There was another pause while he wrote some more. "And then?"

"Then I came out and saw Frank on the floor, tried to check for a pulse, and called 911. The lady told me to get to a safe place, so I hid in the closet until the police came."

"And you didn't hear anything while you were in the closet?"

"Nothing."

"Thank you. That is all very clear. Now, there are few other things I think you might be able to help us with. Do you know if he has any family?"

"No, I don't know of any. He wasn't a very talkative person, but I never heard him mention any family."

"Do you know if anything valuable was taken? Or anything at all?"

"I don't think they took anything. I mean, I didn't search, but nothing was missing that I could tell. Although I thought when the man didn't leave right away that maybe he was looking for something. There was a little bit of noise like he was moving around. But he didn't make much noise—he certainly wasn't ransacking the place—and later I couldn't see anything out of place. And even if it were Matt, he would have looked for the book on the back shelf where I was, I think, not in the closet. I forgot to see if the book was actually in the closet."

"Who is Matt?" The detective looked up from his writing.

"One of my students. Matt Wilkes. He was in the store yesterday and found a book he thought should be in his family." I repeated what Frank had told me.

"And Frank said it sounded like a threat?" said Detective Mason. "He used that word?"

"Yes. And that reminds me—I heard him use that word to someone else last week. On the phone."

That brought up the whole story of the college wanting to buy Frank's building. I reported the phone conversation as accurately as I could.

"Who was he talking to when he was on the phone?"

"I don't know. Probably someone from the Department of Advancement—aren't they the ones that would be trying to get more buildings for the college?"

"It seems likely," the detective agreed. "It shouldn't be too hard to find out. What do you think he meant by saying they were threatening him?"

I shrugged. "I have no idea. It might not have been anything—he was rather a grumpy old man. He might just not have liked what they were saying and threw that into the conversation because he felt like it." For some reason that made my eyes fill up again, and I pulled out a fresh tissue and wiped them. I gave a half-hearted laugh. "I hope I can stop crying before I have to teach tonight."

"You're supposed to teach a class tonight?"

"Yes—English 90. It's the remedial writing class."

Detective Mason looked concerned. "I really think

you ought to go home and rest tonight. You've had quite a shock."

"Oh, I can't! I'd have to cancel class, and evening classes only meet once a week—it's very bad if I cancel one. Do you have more questions? I probably should be getting ready for class pretty soon."

"Right. Well, that's all the questions I have for now. You'll have to sign a statement once it's typed up. I may have more questions for you later. It depends on if we can find any of his family, and if there is anything we discover at the bookstore. Are you all right to wait here for a little while we type this up?"

"Yes—as long as it doesn't take too long."

"We'll do our best. By the way—" He reached into his pocket and pulled out a business card. "If you remember anything else, call me right away, please. Even if it's in the middle of the night. The first day or two after a murder are crucial in solving a case—timing is very important."

"Ok."

He looked at me again. "Are you sure you're all right to go? I know you were driven here in a squad car—I'll arrange to have one take you to where you need to go."

"Thanks, yes, I need to get to campus. I'll be fine."

He got up to leave, paused at the door, and looked back. I thought he was going to say something else, but he changed his mind and left without another word.

It turned out that I *was* ok, but just barely. I made it to class and taught for an hour, but I kept losing concentration and started to stumble over my words. I ended up letting them go home early.

Kim was parked out in front of my apartment building when I got home. I had texted her in the short time I had between the police station and class starting, telling her briefly what had happened and asking her to pray I'd make it through class. Praying wasn't enough for her: she had to come and bring some of my favorite cookies, too.

"I know you probably don't feel like eating," she said, "but whenever you do feel like it, they'll be here for you."

The tears that I had kept under control for the evening came bursting out again, and I got the hug I had needed for hours. She let me cry for a while and then came in my apartment with me, ordered me to go and sit on the couch, and made me a cup of tea.

"Now then," she said, handing it to me, "you sit there and drink it and tell me everything or nothing—whatever you feel like. And then you will go to bed and sleep. Ed says I should stay here with you."

"But Ben and Mia! You know they won't do well without you."

"They'll be fine. They love you, too, and want you to be ok."

"I am ok." I noticed my hand shaking. "Well, almost ok." I started telling her all about it—repeating everything I had told the detective. When I finished, I was exhausted.

"Go to bed," said Kim. "Don't set your alarm—you don't have a class in the morning, do you? No, I didn't think so. Just go. I'm here if you need me."

I went.

I slept better than I had thought I would. I did have one nightmare, but I was able to go back to sleep for the rest of the night. Kim was gone by the time I got out of bed at 10 a.m., but she had left a note ordering me to text her when I got up and tell her how I was. I did so, and then after a mug of hot chocolate, sat down to grade the papers I was supposed to have graded two days ago.

I always start to grade papers with a mixture of emotions. The first one is dread: I know with certitude that I will spend a good amount of time wincing at the mistakes I expressly cautioned against. I battle the suspicion that some of those students will never learn to recognize an incomplete sentence or a non-existent word. And I always start to doubt my teaching ability—surely a better instructor could get better results? I once had a student who wrote me a thank you note at the end of the semester for all I had done to teach him. It would have been heart-warming except that the note read, "Thank you for educationing me."

On the other hand, there is always the hope that some of them will have picked up what I have been trying to communicate: that their thoughts will be more ordered than the last time they put them on paper, more concise, better reasoned, and more carefully researched. And lastly there is the expectation that there will be some amusing mistakes that I can add to my collection. A simple pleasure, but one of the joys of teaching. One, I may say, that I doubt math professors have: I don't think they go to bed chuckling over errors their students made in calculating imaginary numbers. What *do* they talk about at faculty parties?

I graded papers until almost noon. I was slower than usual: my mind kept wandering back to the crime yesterday. I kept hearing that bang over and over. It had been so loud. Why hadn't anyone outside heard it and come running in to see what was wrong? Why hadn't the noise at least alerted people outside to a problem and why hadn't they seen the murderer fleeing from the scene? Perhaps they had; I had no way of knowing. Why hadn't the man used a silencer? There were so many questions, and they were all conspiring to distract me from marking run-on sentences and widowed quotes.

I found that I hadn't left myself enough time to eat before leaving for the college. I changed into some clothes suitable for teaching, grabbed an apple, and headed out to teach American Lit. Morris Creek, the tiny town I live in, is twenty minutes from the college in Wilkester. It's a beautiful drive through farming country. On the other side of Morris Creek is the forest, and while I don't often have time to spend among the trees, I love it when I can. It reminds me of family camping trips when I was little.

The topic that day was one of my favorites; Nathaniel Hawthorne is always fun to teach. Most of the students had slogged through the *Scarlet Letter* in high school and come out the other side with very little besides the firm conviction that the Puritans were hypocritical bad guys. The first half of my lecture consisted of explaining the difference between English and American Puritanism and the changes in Puritanism over time. I followed that up with an explanation of the prevailing attitudes of the times among people of all creeds and finished up with some insights into Hawthorne's perspective. He was, after all, not a Puritan himself. By the end of class, most of the students were fully engaged and we had a good discussion about "The Minister's Black Veil." I even heard a couple of them sigh when I told them time was up. That is the ultimate accolade.

After class, Callie came up and asked if she could speak to me. Callie is one of the brightest students in the class—one of those that you always have in the back of your mind as you are preparing lectures and assignments.

"I was thinking about the paper that's due in a few weeks. You know how we're supposed to write about one work that had influence on others that came after it? I was thinking of writing my paper on Hugh Henry Brackenridge's novel *Modern Chivalry*, and how it influenced the American novels of social criticism."

"That's a great topic!" I said. "You know that we have a first edition of *Modern Chivalry* in the library here, right?"

"Yes, and that's what I wanted to speak to you about. Do you know how I can get in to see it? I tried to ask at the library, but they said a professor had to arrange it."

"That's right. I just need to let the library know and go in with you. Would you be able to come in early before class on Friday? If you meet me at the library at twelve we'll have time to see the book before class starts."

"That would be great!" she said, just as my cell phone rang.

"No problem," I said, and waited until she headed out the door before I answered it. I didn't recognize the number.

"Hello?"

"Hello, Miss Peters? This is Detective Mason. I was wondering if you could come back to the police station. We have a few more questions for you—some things we think you might be able to help us with."

"Sure," I said. "I've just finished class—I can be there in a few minutes."

"Perfect. See you soon."

———

I reported to the front desk of the police station, and

one of the officers took me back to a room like the one I had made my statement in before. Detective Mason was there, sitting at a side table, working at an ancient computer. I looked twice at the computer. "That looks like Frank's computer!" I said.

"It is," said the detective. He stood up and shook my hand. He looked exhausted. "You look much better today," he said. "That is—" he flushed a little. "You look more rested."

"I am, thank you. You look—" I was going to say "terrible" but stopped myself just in time. "You look tired."

He smiled fully at that. "I am. Very tired. It's all right—I've just been on duty for a long time. Anyway, about the computer. It's part of the evidence from the crime scene. We took it from the bookstore to see if it might help us find out who would want to kill Frank."

"You hacked into his computer?" I asked.

"We would have if we'd needed to, but as it turned out he didn't even have it password protected."

I nodded. "Sounds like Frank."

"He seems to have used his email just for business purposes. We haven't found a personal email account. Someone may have stolen his home computer because we can't find one. And we can't find a cell phone."

"He didn't have one," I said. "Either one. He didn't like technology. He only used that computer for work because it's nearly impossible to run any kind of business without it."

The detective groaned.

"What's wrong?" I asked.

"My job just became a lot more difficult. It's harder to find information about people who are more or less off the grid. If we have a cell phone to look at, we can see who they called and who called them immediately, without getting records from the phone company. We can see where they went, what kind of alerts were set up on their phones, who they took pictures of, what kinds of apps they had—all kinds of stuff."

"I see. I don't think there will be anything like that with Frank."

"No. Well, we need to look at the emails that we do have to see if there is anything there that might be a possible motive for murder. Most of them seem to be business enquiries about buying or selling books. We found a few that weren't, and we actually printed one out that we want to ask you about, but we thought it might be a good idea if you scrolled through the last few weeks' worth of emails, just to see if there was anything that jumped out at you."

I was given a seat at the computer, and I dutifully looked at every email for the past two months. It didn't take too long. Frank's inbox was completely given over to the business—unlike my email that fills up with those cheery weekly notifications from companies that I once bought something from or social media platforms who want to alert me every time a contact of mine does anything. I recognized most of the names as buyers who regularly ordered books from the store or suppliers that send us books. Even the ones that didn't look familiar turned out to be routine communications.

"I don't see anything unusual at all," I said. "I'm sorry."

"Could you also look at the 'sent' folder?"

"All right." I opened it and started reading emails. "This is unusual," I said, pointing to one. "I didn't know Frank was in communication with this man."

Detective Mason looked over my shoulder. "Yes, we wondered if that was unusual. It's the one that we printed out for you."

The email was to G. Weatherill and read,

Dear Dr. Weatherill,

I have come by some evidence that a document that you authenticated is, in fact, a forgery. I have not yet told anyone of this, as I am not certain who should be told. The evidence I have shows that it was very cleverly done, and I'm sure no blame can attach to you in thinking it was above board. I would appreciate if you would communicate with me and tell me if the police ought to be the first ones to know, or the owner, or if you yourself would like to look into it and perhaps re-assess the document. All is safe for now, and I will await further instructions before I take any more steps.

Sincerely,
Frank Delaney

"He didn't tell you anything about this?"

"Not about finding evidence. He did ask me about forgeries last week…" I looked at the date of the email. "Yes, it was the day he sent the email. He asked me how you would recognize a forgery. I asked if he had bought a book he thought was a forgery and he said no, but he didn't say anything more than that. I suppose it would make sense for him to contact Professor Weatherill if he thought there might be a problem."

"Do you know Dr. Weatherill?"

"Not well. He was a professor of mine when I was a college student, but he's well known all over the country— one of the top experts for authenticating manuscripts that turn up. I know he works with Sotheby's and other auction houses. He's done work for the Smithsonian, too. I'm not surprised he hasn't responded to the email."

"Which college does he teach at?"

"I don't know anymore. He was teaching at UCSC when I was there, but he left before I graduated and I haven't kept track of where he went."

"UCSC—that's in California, right?"

"Yes, University of California, Santa Clarita. But as I said, he could be anywhere now. I'm sure he'd be easy to find—he's quite famous."

"Thank you, that's very helpful. Are there any other sent emails that are unusual?"

I continued scanning. "Not really. Most of them are replies to emails sent by other people. There are a few that originated with Frank, but they are all to people he normally did business with. If he had wanted to communicate with someone about a private or sensitive matter, he would have written a paper letter and sent it through the post office."

"Why do you think he didn't do that with Dr. Weatherill?"

"He probably couldn't find a physical address for him. Frank wasn't the best researcher."

"Thank you. I have a few more questions for you—we can sit down over here at the other end of the table, away from the computer. Now, we found this handwritten note at the crime scene. It was in the trash can. We wondered if you knew anything about it, or maybe recognized the handwriting."

He handed me a note that had been crumpled and then smoothed out. It read,

"Mr. Delaney,

We know the deed you have for your building is a forgery. If you sell the building to us, this never has to come to light. Call me at your earliest convenience."

K

"Wow," I said. "Is that the forgery Frank was talking about?"

"I'm not sure," said Detective Mason.

"And wouldn't that be illegal? I mean, if you buy something that doesn't really belong to the other person, isn't that compounding a felony?"

"Not exactly, especially if it was an ancestor of the person who sold it that committed the fraud. The statute of limitations would have run out decades ago. However, you could still be sued by the people who truly owned the property and have to give it back. Do you recognize the handwriting?"

"No, not at all."

"Do you know anything about the ownership of the building? Did Frank ever say anything to you about the ownership of the building?"

I tried to think back to the conversations I'd had with Frank. "He wasn't one to chat about his personal life, even if you asked him questions. I remember once I asked him if he had started the bookstore, because it seemed such an unlikely thing for him to do. He wasn't much of a reader and didn't even know that much about literature or old books. He said that his grandfather had bought the building and used it as some kind of store. A hardware store, maybe? I know he said his father had it as a hardware store, but I don't know if it started off that way. It was Frank who turned it into a bookstore, but I've never found out why."

"I know you said the college wanted to buy the bookstore, but had you heard of anyone else wanting to buy it?"

"No, never, but it is in a good location, and it's possible there was someone else who wanted it. Frank certainly didn't tell me everything."

There was silence for a minute as he wrote down what I'd said. "I'd also like to ask you about your student, Matt Wilkes. Do you know him well?"

"No, not really. This is the first class of mine that he's taken. He seems to be a good student—hard-working and conscientious."

"Did he ever say anything or write anything that you know of which would make you think he was prone to violence?"

"No, not that I can think of."

"All right, I have one other thing to ask you about. If you could wait here for a minute, please." He left the room and was back in less than a minute, carrying a book. He put it in front of me. "Do recognize this?"

"Yes, that's the diary of Matthew Wilkes."

"The one your student said he wanted to buy from Mr. Delaney?"

"Yes."

"Thank you. I think there are no further questions at this time. You have been extremely helpful."

I sighed. "I don't feel like I have been helpful. I don't seem to know much of anything you've asked about."

He looked at me again and smiled. He really had a charming smile. I wondered if he used charm on suspects to get them to talk.

"Don't worry about it, Miss Peters. You couldn't possibly have known the answers to most of my questions, and the ones you did know saved us a lot of time."

"Thanks," I said. "Would you mind if I asked you a question? I've been wondering about something."

"Sure, go ahead."

"I was wondering about how loud the gunshot was. Why didn't he use a silencer? And why didn't anyone outside hear the shot?"

The detective leaned back in his chair. "He probably did use a silencer, or suppressor as they're also called. I know in movies it makes the gun actually silent, but in real life even guns with silencers are pretty loud."

"Oh!"

"And people did hear the shot. At least, a few of them did. There wasn't much foot traffic at the time, though, and when you're indoors and just hear one muffled sound, it's hard to know exactly what it is or where it came from."

"No one saw someone running away?"

"No. And if the culprit walked calmly away, no one would connect them with the loud sound."

"No surveillance cameras in the area, I suppose?"

He smiled again. "No, there weren't."

"Well, I do hope you catch him." That sounded lame when I said it aloud.

He wasn't smiling at all when he said, "So do we."

CHAPTER 4

By the time I left the police station I was incredibly hungry. It was now almost three-thirty, and there was a sandwich place I'd heard about just down the street. I figured it was as good a time as any to try it out.

It was a colorful, well-lit, and clean little restaurant. It had once been an old-school diner, and the owners had kept the original long counter with stools you could perch on while you ate there. There were booths, too, of course, but I opted for the seat at the far end of the counter. One of my least favorite things is sitting alone in a restaurant. Everyone else always seems to be eating with other people, and the empty seat across the table at my booth makes me feel conspicuous. Then there's always the question of where to look. My gaze tends to lock in on other diners, even if I'm not conscious of it, and when they swivel around and catch me absent-mindedly staring at them, I am, as Dickens would say, covered in confusion. My solution for this is to pull out a book and read while I eat. Yes, I know, how very spinsterish. If I were one of those personable, outgoing, winsome people, I would be able to strike up conversations with servers and other diners and have a clutch of new friends by the time I paid the check. But I'm not.

I ordered the Classic Club sandwich and opened

Romola. It's not a favorite of mine—in fact, I can only take small doses of it, which is why I keep it with me to read when I'm stuck someplace like a waiting room or restaurant. But I challenged myself to read everything written by George Eliot this year, and I will not be beaten by a dull book.

I only dimly noticed when someone sat down at the counter a couple seats away from me. It wasn't until the words, "Hello, Miss Peters" registered that I looked up.

It was the detective.

"Oh, hello, Detective Mason."

He waved his hand. "I'm off duty now. Just call me Todd."

"Oh! Ok. And I'm Katrina." And then came one of those awkward pauses that I never know what to do with. Should I go back to reading? Or would that seem rude? If I close the book instead, might he think I'm expecting him to talk to me throughout the meal? I'd hate to seem presumptuous. I hovered there with the book still open but not looking at it.

"I didn't mean to interrupt your reading," he said.

"You're not, really. I just keep this with me for when I have to wait."

"That's interesting," he said. "Most people just look at their phones."

"I know. I'm odd." I said it with a smile so he wouldn't think I was begging to be contradicted.

"No, I don't think so. Unusual, maybe, but definitely not odd." The charming smile came into play again.

It flashed across my mind that he might be flirting with me. Probably not, because I'm not the kind of woman that gets flirted with except by desperate men that would flirt with anyone, and he was definitely not that kind of man. I made the quick decision to be on the safe side. If you throw church into a flirty conversation, you can count on the banter dying out within the next minute.

"Well, if you ask my preschool Sunday School class if I'm odd, they will assure you that I am. Ever since I told them that I *like* broccoli, they think I'm weird. But since I give them chocolate on their birthdays instead of broccoli, they love me anyway."

He actually chuckled. "I'll bet they're lots of fun to teach."

The waitress put my food down in front of me and then turned to Todd and took his order. I took advantage of the moment to bow my head and say a silent grace. If he was in any doubt about my religiosity, that would remove it.

When I raised my head again and started eating he asked, "So, do you enjoy being a professor?"

"Most of the time, yes. It has its tedious moments, but I think you get that with any profession."

"Very true. I've always wondered—is being a college professor accurately portrayed in TV and movies? I mean, I was a college student, so I know what classrooms are like, but I don't know what goes on behind the scenes."

"I think it's mostly accurate. Not that there are very many shows with a professor as the protagonist. I don't think it's considered very exciting work. I mean, if there is a professor in a show, he either spends his free time helping the FBI or chasing Nazis through the Middle East. The actual teaching part doesn't really come into the story. Let alone grading papers."

"That's probably the tedious part of your profession. Those parts always get left out of movies. Like lawyers—I have a friend who's a lawyer and he says ninety percent of his time is spent reviewing documents, reading every single word of contracts. You never see that on television. He thought it would be more like Matlock."

I laughed. "I know. I have friends who are foster parents, and when I see a show where a bunch of newly-adopted older kids fit into their new surroundings with just one little frustrated outburst, I have to roll my eyes."

"I can imagine. It's probably like watching cop shows when you are a detective. Sometimes you can't even enjoy the story because it's all so inaccurate."

"Like what? I know you told me about silencers not really making the guns silent."

The waitress put his BLT down in front of him and he thanked her and then said to me, "Excuse me." *And bowed his head.*

It was only for a moment, giving me just enough time to veil my surprise by taking a big bite of my sandwich. As if handsome single detectives that seemed to want to chat with me and might possibly be Christians were a common thing in my life.

"There are lots of things they get wrong," he said after his silent prayer. "For example, they have uniformed policemen standing around the crime scene, drawing conclusions about the psychology of the murderer while twenty SCIs in hazmat suits scuttle around them. Or they have someone use their breath to blow open an evidence bag before putting in some fibers they found—totally contaminating it, of course. Or their computer checks take mere minutes to get all the background of a suspect, when in reality it would take days or weeks. For example, we still don't have the phone records for Mr. Delaney, and probably won't for a few more days. And never, ever, do they show the hours of paperwork you have to do. I could go on and on."

"That must be very frustrating."

"Yes, well, I don't actually have that much time for

watching TV. Especially when I'm in the middle of a case like this one."

"Will you be able to get some sleep now? You said you're off duty."

"I'll go home and sleep after I eat. There's not much I can do until tomorrow morning anyway. We need to find Mr. Delaney's will, if he made one, and get more information about his family and a few things like that. We have guys going through his house now, looking for information."

I smiled. "That part *does* sound like a detective show."

"True. And sometimes it really is as exciting as those shows make it seem. Not that often, but sometimes."

I was pretty much done with my meal and was wondering if I ought to stay until he finished eating and risk him thinking I was spending more time with him because I was after him, or if I ought to leave now and risk him thinking I was dying to get away from him because I didn't enjoy his company. Neither would be true, of course, but once having embarked on that line of thought, I couldn't figure out what I would have done if I didn't care what he thought. Overthinking a situation has always been a hobby of mine.

"Do you mind if I ask you where you go to church?" he said suddenly.

I may have blinked in surprise. "Faith Community Church here in Wilkester. And you?"

"A few different places. Usually Highview Baptist in Tacoma."

"I see." That didn't bode well. Not being committed to one church can point to a lack of spiritual health. Well, maybe it had to do with his schedule or something.

My phone rang. "Excuse me," I said to Todd as I tapped the answer button.

"Aunt Katrina? It's Deirdre." That's Kim and Ed's teenaged daughter. "Mom asked me to call you and ask if you are free to come over and help—Ben ran away again, farther this time, and they're out looking for him. Mia is scared and Josh is at practice and I don't know if I can make dinner by myself in case they're gone a long time."

"Of course I'll come," I said. "I'll be there soon. Hang in there."

I hung up and turned to Todd. "I've got to go. There's a bit of a crisis with one of the foster kids."

"A serious crisis?"

"Too early to tell, but probably not. I'm going to help with the other kids." I put my book into my purse and stood up. "It was nice chatting with you," I said. "I enjoyed that."

"Same here," he said. "Hope everything goes well."

I walked the length of the counter to pay my bill at the far end. As I pushed open the restaurant door to leave, I glanced back. Todd was watching me, and he waved and smiled again. Does it sound hackneyed to say that I felt a warm glow? Probably so, but it's still the best phrase to describe my feelings as I drove to the Coles'.

As I parked my car in front of the house, Mia came running out to meet me. There is nothing as delightful as a small child running to you with arms open and calling your name.

"Aunt Katrina! You came!"

I hugged her and took her hand, and she chattered all the way into the house.

"Guess how much two plus two is?"

"Ummmm," I pretended to be thinking hard.

"It's *four*! I learned it at school today and I haven't forgotten yet. And you know how many hearts octopuses have? Guess!"

"One?"

"No! It's three!"

"Really? I don't think I ever knew that. You're such a smart girl!"

She giggled. "Am I smarter than you?"

"I'll tell you this: you knew that an octopus has three hearts and you're only five. And I'm forty-one and I didn't know that until today!"

Mia jumped up the steps of the front porch happily. Deirdre met me at the door. She was tall for her fifteen years, and she was twisting her long blond hair, as she did whenever she was worried.

"Any word?" I asked her.

"Not yet. Mom called a little while ago and said that someone thought they had seen him near Douglass Park. They're going to head that way and see if he's there. If not, they'll probably have to call the police."

"Oh dear. Let's hope they find him soon. Now, where are the boys?"

"Sam is outside brushing Molly, and Josh isn't back from practice yet. His friend is going to drop him off."

I led the way to the back yard, where thirteen-year-old Sam was brushing the St. Bernard. Molly got to her feet when she saw me and shoved her slobbery nose into my side. Her slowly wagging tail brushed back and forth against Mia's face, which made her giggle again.

"How's it going, Sam?"

"Fine." Sam is a boy of few words.

"So, what are we making for dinner?" I asked Deirdre.

"Mom left the ingredients for chicken divan out. I might need a little help to make it."

The phone rang inside the house. Mia rushed inside to answer it. We could hear her from where we were.

"HellothisistheColes'residencehowcanIhelpyou?" she said in one breath. I hoped whoever was on the other end could tell that it was English; there was a sporting chance it could be mistaken for Latvian.

"Hi, Mommy! … Ok." She raised her voice. "Deirdre! Mom wants to talk to you!"

Deidre went to the phone. "Hey, Mom…Yes, she just got here… Yep, they're fine…Oh, good…. Ok….Ok, I'll tell her. Bye." She came outside again. "Mom says they found him at the park, but he's still upset and won't come with them. They'll have to stay there with him until he's ready to go."

I nodded. They could hardly drag a kicking and screaming seven-year-old through the park and force him into a car without someone calling Child Services on them.

"Right," I said. "Mia, why don't you stay out here with Sam and play on the trampoline? Sam, can you keep an eye on her while you finish brushing Molly? Deirdre, you and I can start fixing dinner."

I got Deirdre to start chopping the broccoli while I cooked the chicken and made the sauce.

"Do you know what upset Ben?" I asked.

"His birthmother didn't show up for her time with him yesterday."

It was too old a story to need any comment. I felt a surge of frustration against the system that kept him legally tied to a woman who could not care for him enough to see him just once a month. In time he would probably be released from that forced connection and be able to be securely placed in a loving family. Until then, he would feel her rejection of him over and over, every time she missed a meeting or failed to fulfil a requirement the judge had set for her to regain custody of her son.

"How's your art class going?" I asked. "It's through

that Christian arts program, right? On Saturdays?"

"It's good. I like the teacher—he's a really awesome artist." She glanced at me out of the corner of her eye. "Aunt Katrina, would you go on a blind date?"

"I have done it—once or twice."

She grinned.

"Now wait a minute," I said. "I don't go out with just anyone."

"Oh, I know," she said. "He'd have to be a believer."

"Not just that. We'd have to have mutual friends that knew both of us pretty well for me to consider it. And I don't want to marry someone who's been married before, and most men my age have been."

Deirdre's enthusiasm deflated. "Oh. Why not?"

"I don't want to be someone's second choice."

"But what if his wife died? What if he didn't choose you first because he didn't know you then?"

"He'd still have memories of his first wife. He'd always be comparing me with her. I don't like the idea of that kind of competition."

"It's not a *competition*, like where you'd get a prize for being a better wife."

"No, of course it's not that kind of competition. I don't know how to explain it." I gave my full concentration to the sauce I was stirring on the stove. "If you've finished chopping, we can put that broccoli in the steamer for just a few minutes."

"I know what it is," Deirdre said as she transferred the little green florets to the steamer basket. "You want to marry someone who will say 'There will never be anyone for me but you,' like Anne and Gilbert Blythe. You want a Jane Austen novel kind of marriage."

"Well, maybe," I said. "Yes, I suppose it's something like that. I'd just rather not be married at all than be in a situation where I'd always wonder if he was thinking about his former wife, and if he would be wishing he could have her back instead of having me."

Deirdre rolled her eyes. "No one who was married to you would wish they were married to someone else. You would be a *great* wife! Especially to my art teacher."

"Well, thank you. You're very sweet. Is he the one you wanted to set me up with?"

She nodded. "His wife died a couple years ago. Are you sure you won't consider it? What if *God* wants you to marry someone whose wife died?"

"He won't," I said glibly. "I think this chicken is done. Would you mind chopping it while I grate the cheese?" And then before she could revert back to the topic of potential marriage partners, I asked her about her homework.

"Yes, I have plenty," she said. "There's a test tomorrow in history. Kelsey is coming over tonight to study with me."

"Kelsey? Is that the one who was here a few weeks ago who wanted to give you a makeover instead of working on that English project?"

"Yeah. She's not really a fan of studying hard. I'm trying to help her because her grades are really low."

"Maybe letting her fail would be a good wakeup call."

"I don't think so. She knows she'll get accepted and get a full scholarship to Wilkester College no matter what her grades are, so she doesn't care about trying very hard."

"Why is she so sure she'll get in?"

"She's a Wilkes. It goes with being part of the family."

"Is she! I didn't know that. Here, get the broccoli out of the steamer and we'll layer it all together."

When the casserole was assembled and in the oven,

we started working on the salad.

"Hey, does your friend Kelsey have an older brother named Matt?"

"No, but she has a cousin named Matt. He goes to the college now."

"Yes, I think he must be the one who's in one of my classes. So you mean he's gotten a guaranteed place in the college and a scholarship on top of it?"

"And a guaranteed job at the end of it."

"At that real estate company? What is it—Wilkes Group Real Estate or something like that?"

"That's right. Some of the perks they get for being a Wilkes are because of the family businesses, and some of them are in the town bylaws from a long time ago. Or the college rules. The person who started the college was a Wilkes, and so were all the original trustees."

"That hardly seems fair in the twenty-first century. You'd think there would be some kind of law against preferential treatment."

Deirdre shrugged. "I'm sure that, officially, it's all equal opportunity, but things just seem to work in their favor."

The phone rang again. This time I answered it.

"Hi, Katrina? We're on our way back with Ben. We should be there in about twenty minutes."

"Great! You'll be just in time for dinner then."

I hung up the phone and reflected that I might just have it in me to run a household with a couple foster children in it. Dinner had been made, all the kids were gainfully occupied—except for Josh, who was due home any minute, and I'd been able to discuss a grown-up topic like marriage with a teenager. I felt competent.

That feeling was crushed a few minutes later when Mia came running in, screaming because she had found an

49

ant crawling on her leg. Then Sam, who had taken Molly for a walk down the street without informing me, came back to discover that he hadn't quite latched the gate, and the little terrier named Houdini had gotten out—again. Josh arrived home on the heels of this discovery, and as soon as his friend drove off, realized he had left his school backpack in the gym. Ed and Kim arrived to find a scene of total chaos.

Of course, everything was set to rights as soon as the parents started managing it all. Mia was soothed in record time, Ed took Josh with him in the car to go back to the gym to get the backpack and look for Houdini along the way, and I meekly set the table for dinner.

It was a quiet meal. Mia and Ben appeared to have exhausted themselves emotionally for the day, and the teens seemed absorbed with their own thoughts. It wasn't until Kim and I were cleaning up that I realized I hadn't really thought about the murder all evening. It had been a welcome break.

"Is the rest of your week looking really busy?" asked Kim.

"Not really. I've just got to catch up on all the things I didn't do while spending those hours at the police station in the last couple days. Thank goodness they won't need me anymore. I really have to finish grading those papers tonight, and I want to prepare for Monday's library book club meeting. And one of my authors is about to send me something to edit."

"Got time for a blind date?" There was a twinkle in Kim's eye.

"Not you too!" I exclaimed.

"What do you mean, me too? Who else is trying to set you up?"

"Deirdre. Her art teacher."

"So she got to you first. Well, what did you say?"

"You know I don't go out with men that have been married before."

"I was hoping you had changed your mind on that."

"Well, I haven't. If I can't have the kind of relationship that I'm comfortable with, then I'd rather be single."

"Still waiting for Captain Wentworth, eh?" She struck a dramatic pose. "'I have loved none but you.'"

I flicked a dishtowel at her.

"But what if *God* wants you to marry a widower?" she persisted.

"I can see where Deirdre gets her thought processes," I said.

"You haven't answered the question."

"Ok, yes, if God wants me to marry a widower, I will. Satisfied?"

"Satisfied."

"But I'm still not going on a blind date with the art teacher. And God will have to put a message in neon lights in the sky before I'll be convinced He's asking me to marry him!"

CHAPTER 5

I ended my Thursday English Comp class with a reminder that Punctuation Presentations were due the following week and then gathered up my teaching notes while the students who had been procrastinating for the last five weeks groaned in near-unison. Two of them came up to talk to me about an extension as the others filed out of the classroom, and I had just finished talking to the second one when I noticed Detective Mason waiting outside my door. I damped down the little happy flutter I felt on seeing him.

"Good afternoon, Miss Peters. Would you mind coming down to the station now? We have a few more questions for you."

"Uh, sure. Should I meet you there?"

"No, you can ride along with me." He seemed less approachable than he had been the day before—more business-like. Of course, he was on duty now.

The ride to the police station was short and more silent than I would have expected. The detective seemed so formal that I was too intimidated to try to make conversation. I began to wonder if I had been too friendly yesterday, and he was doing his best to discourage my attentions. If that was it, he was doing a splendid job.

I was taken to an interrogation room and asked to sit

down. Detective Mason sat across from me, as he had previously, but before he could ask me any questions we were joined by another man, introduced as Detective Ortega. If anything, Mr. Ortega was the friendlier of the two. This time there was a recording device set up to record my answers.

"Miss Peters, do you know anything about the contents of Mr. Delaney's will?"

"No. I wasn't even sure he had a will. I mean, I would have thought that he did, but he never mentioned it."

"What was your relationship to Frank Delaney?"

"Just a friend. Hardly even that. I would say he was more of a colleague, but I didn't really work for the bookstore. More like a close acquaintance. I never saw him outside the store."

"You were not related at all?"

"No," I said, increasingly surprised by this string of questions. Did they think we looked alike or something? "I never heard of him or saw him until I walked into his bookstore a couple years ago when I first moved to Washington."

"Do you own a gun, Dr. Peters?" That was Detective Ortega. It jolted me a bit, because I don't usually go by "Dr." outside of the classroom.

"No."

"Do you know how to shoot? Are you familiar with guns?"

"Not really. One time my brother took me to a shooting range, just for fun, but it's not really my thing."

"Do you have access to your brother's guns?"

"No. He lives in California, for one thing. And I don't even know if he still has his gun, let alone where he keeps it." It was all very weird—almost like I was a suspect.

"Did you ever argue with Mr. Delaney?" This came

from Detective Mason.

"No, never. I don't think I was his favorite person, but he didn't seem to like many people. I'd say he tolerated me better than most. I don't even know what we would have argued about."

The two detectives exchanged a glance, and I saw Todd give a tiny nod.

"Dr. Peters," said Detective Ortega, "did you know that Mr. Delaney was going to leave you the bookstore in his will?"

My mouth fell open. "What?"

"We found his will. You are named as the beneficiary of his business. He left you the store—the building, the books, and the business."

"But *why*? I didn't even know him very well."

"We were hoping you could tell us," said Detective Ortega.

I shook my head. "I have no idea. I never gave him the slightest hint that I would want to own a bookstore—because I don't, really."

"Did you ever mention that fact to anyone at the college? Or anyone at all?"

"What, that I don't want to own a bookstore? I don't think so. I mean, it's never come up. If someone had asked me if I ever wanted to own a bookstore, I would have told them no, but I can't remember anyone ever asking me that."

"Do you think you might sell it, then?"

"Gosh, I don't know. Possibly. I mean, I'll have to think about it." *Nifty,* I thought. *Another item to add to the list of things I have to decide about.*

Detective Mason spoke up. "It's just possible that someone who wanted the building knew you would be getting it if something happened to Mr. Delaney. They might have thought you would sell it to them if it were yours."

The thought was a bit bewildering. "That seems like a very complicated motive. Like something that would be in a movie about the mafia—someone being bumped off for the inheritance." I said it in a light-hearted tone, but the detectives didn't smile back.

"Do you have any connection with someone in organized crime?" asked Detective Ortega.

"Uh, no." I felt like one of those missionaries that get accused of spying and plotting to overthrow a foreign government. It was all I could do not to blurt out "You've got to be kidding!"

"Thank you," said Detective Mason. He reached over and turned off the recording device. "If you would wait here for a moment," he said, as both men scooted back their chairs and stood up, "I'll be back with you shortly." They left the room together.

It was the strangest thing: I was starting to feel guilty. Like I had actually done something criminal. I felt the urge to apologize for something—anything! But I couldn't think of what I could possibly have done wrong. Would they arrest me for murdering Frank? I supposed I could see their point. I was the one who reported finding the body, after all. But why wait until now?

Detective Mason came back in and sat down. He looked at my face and the faint smile came back.

"Don't worry," he said. "You're not in trouble."

I gave a sigh of relief. "I'm so glad. I felt like I'd done something illegal."

"Sorry. We had to ask those questions. You were the first person on the scene, and when we found out that the bookstore was willed to you, it provided a motive, and we had to rule you out as a suspect."

"And have you ruled me out?"

"Yes."

"That's good. Could I ask a question?"

"Sure."

"How did you know that I was telling you the truth? I mean, I could have said I didn't know Frank before, but what if I was lying? How would you know?"

"I wouldn't—not without doing a lot of research. But usually people who would lie about that would lie about other things, too. It's very hard to tell a long, consistent lie, and people who are lying usually end up with discrepancies in their stories. Also, not many Sunday school teachers are guilty of murder."

"Yes, but I might have been lying about that."

"You weren't. I found out one of the administrators at the college is also one of the elders at your church. It turned out he was also your friend. He was able to vouch for you, and to confirm that you do teach Sunday school."

"You talked to Ed?"

Detective Mason nodded.

"You mean that conversation yesterday—you weren't just being chatty and friendly? You were investigating me?"

"No—no, not at all. I was just being friendly. But when the will came to light this morning, and protocol dictated that we consider you a potential suspect, I remembered what you said and used the information to clear you more quickly." He leaned forward slightly. "Frankly, Miss Peters, I never considered you a viable suspect. But the police chief couldn't just take my confidence that you are a genuine Christian as rock-solid evidence that you were innocent. But he could agree that your character being vouched for by a reliable witness, no police record or evidence against you, plus the lack of a strong motive meant that we really had no reason to think you were our criminal."

"So you didn't think I was guilty even before you talked to me today?"

"No."

I must have looked puzzled.

"That surprises you?"

"You seemed so stern today. I felt like you really did think I was guilty."

"Some of that was just protocol in interrogating someone."

"What was the other part?"

"I knew you might feel hurt if you were accused, and I was dreading you going through that questioning, especially when I knew it wasn't really necessary to establish your innocence."

"Oh." The thought that he felt bad for me ignited that little flutter again. I smacked it down. "Did you find out if Frank had any family? He must not have, if he left the store to me."

"It seems he had a cousin that he was estranged from. We haven't had a chance to talk to him yet."

"I see. Well, let me know…" I broke off. "I guess the police don't tell suspects—or witnesses, I suppose—what they find out. But if Frank left me the store, I'd like to know what his cousin says about it. Maybe he knows why Frank turned it into a bookstore in the first place, or something. I like to know the history of things."

Todd sat there pondering for a minute. "I think it might be valuable to have you here when we talk to the cousin. He's not a suspect at all, and between the two of you we might be able to figure out some things. Would that be all right? I can't require you to come, but it might be helpful."

"I'd like that," I said.

"Would you be free tomorrow?"

"Well, I have class from one to two, but otherwise I'm free. Oh, I do have to meet a student at twelve tomorrow, too."

"Would you be able to come at three?"

"Sure."

"Great! I'll drive you back to campus now."

The ride back to campus was much more sociable than the ride away from it had been.

"By the way," I said, "How long will it take before the bookstore is actually mine? I mean, until I can go in there?"

"It will probably take three to six weeks once probate is granted before the bookstore and property are registered in your name. There is a lawyer who was named as the executor, and he'll take care of all that administration. Why do you ask?"

"I wondered if I could go in and see if there was anything missing or messed up."

"I imagine you could do that at any time. It will be yours eventually, and the police and forensics team have finished with it. Do you have a key?"

"I do, actually. Are all the police seals gone and everything?"

"Yes, it's all cleared up."

"The police cleaned up the…the blood?"

"No. Actually, that's the owner's job."

"But he's…oh. I'm the owner." I felt a little ill. I couldn't imagine having to go in there and see the spot on the carpet where Frank had lost his life, let alone scrub it out.

"There are companies you can contract to clean up a crime scene."

"Are there? But they're probably expensive."

"Not too much for a small job like that. But do you have a friend who'd be willing? Maybe some guys from your church?"

"Maybe. I'll ask around."

Todd dropped me off at the front of the campus. "See you tomorrow," he said with a grin that made me think he was looking forward to it. I think I might have felt a warm glow at that, but my mind was in too much of a whirl for it to really register.

Instead of going straight to my car, I walked through campus to the path that led to the back of Frank's store. I didn't want to go in, but I wanted to see it, now that it belonged to me. I've never owned any kind of building before. My friends had often joked about the bookshelves in my apartment looking like a library or a bookstore, but that was nothing to this. I wondered how many thousand volumes were in the store. All mine now. It wasn't exciting as much as it was just odd.

There is an opening in the wall that forms the boundary between the college and the bookstore. I suspect Frank had never put a gate on in because it made it easier for the professors and students to come and while away an idle hour in his store and find something to buy. When I reached the gap, I saw someone at the back door of the store. I paused to watch. They seemed to be trying to do something with the lock on the door.

The killer returning for whatever he missed the first time? Part of me wanted to turn around and run. Instead, I slipped behind the wall to think. The killer (if it was him) couldn't know I was a kind of witness to the murder. Therefore, I didn't run a huge risk if I was seen. Unless the murderer thought that being seen at all was a huge risk to his being identified. But if that were the case, why would he be fooling around with a door in broad daylight, with nothing to stop someone using this path and seeing him?

And if it *was* the murderer, I should do whatever I could to see who it was. The police seemed to have no idea who it might be, and someone trying to get into the locked building was probably as close as they had come to a lead.

Then again, it might just be an ordinary thief. A thief that was trying to rob *my store*. I peeked around the corner again. The guy was still at it, hunched over and fiddling with something near the door handle. It looked like he was trying to pick the lock.

All at once he stood up and shoved whatever was in his hand into his pocket. He turned around and headed in my direction. He was looking at the ground, but I saw his face.

"Matt?"

He executed a perfect start.

"Professor Peters! Um, hi."

I decided not to let on that I had seen him try to break and enter.

"Did you need something from the store? It's closed now."

"Yes, I figured that out. Do you know when it might be open?"

"No. Not for a while now. The owner died."

"Really?" I didn't like how Matt wasn't meeting my eyes.

"Yes, really."

"That's too bad. I was wondering…uh…I think I left something in the store the last time I was in there. I just wanted to get it back."

"What did you leave there?"

"A book. A textbook."

"Well, if you tell me the name of it, I'll have a look

around for it when I'm able to go in."

"Are they going to sell all the books then? Can people go in and buy them?"

"I'm not sure," I said truthfully. "I don't know what is going to happen to the books. What's the textbook I should look for?"

"Oh, never mind. It doesn't matter. I'd better get going. See you in class, Professor." He walked back down the path I had come by.

I found myself shaking a little when he had gone. "My poor nerves," I murmured, and was annoyed to realize I sounded just like Mrs. Bennet.

It wasn't until I made it back to my car that it came to me that I ought to call Todd. I dug through my purse until I found the card he had given me. I dialed the number and concentrated on taking slow, deep breaths while it rang.

"Detective Mason."

"Um, hello, Detective. This is Katrina Peters. Something happened that I thought I should tell you about."

"Yes?"

"I saw someone trying to get into the bookstore, doing something with the lock. It was Matt Wilkes, my student. He gave up and started walking away and then I talked to him. He just said he'd left a textbook in there, but I think he was lying."

"Are you still there at the college?"

"Yes, in the parking lot. In my car."

"Stay there. I'll be right there."

"What?" I said. But he had already hung up.

I only had to wait about ten minutes before he came. I got out of the car and walked with him to the back of the bookstore. He looked carefully at the lock Matt had been

61

fooling with.

"See anything?" I said.

"No, but then I'd be surprised if I did see something. Lock picks don't leave marks on the face of the lock. The forensics lab could tell from the inside of the lock whether the lock was picked, but since you actually saw him try to unlock the door with something, and since he didn't get in, there's really no need to prove it. But you're sure it was Matt Wilkes you saw?"

"Positive."

"That means there's something in there he wants pretty badly."

"All I can think of is that diary, which is still at the police station, right?"

"Right. But his actions seem pretty extreme just to get a family diary back."

"He asked me if the books would be sold, and I told him I didn't know. Maybe he'll try to get it that way."

"Hm. Unless he is the murderer and left something behind that he wants to retrieve."

"Wouldn't the crime scene people have found it?"

"Probably, if they saw something that seemed out of place. But if whatever it was looked like it might belong there, they wouldn't notice it."

"Oh."

"Perhaps *you* ought to go in and see if you see anything out of place."

"Now?" I shrank from the idea of going in and seeing the…seeing the spot where Frank had died.

"If you can bear to. Once a cleaning crew has come, it might be too late. And of course someone might try again to get in there."

"We could post a guard, couldn't we? Like a policeman on a stakeout?" Into my mind flashed a picture of Todd inviting me to sit in a car on a stakeout with him. That might be fun.

"I don't think the chief would think we have the resources to expend on that possibility. You might think about getting a security camera, though."

"I'm sure that would cost a bundle." I contemplated the possibility for a moment and then dismissed it. "Anyway, I couldn't get it installed today."

"No, you couldn't. Would you be ok looking inside?"

I found myself trembling a little. "Do I have to go in by myself?"

"No, no, I'll go with you. I ought to be there if you find anything."

I squared my shoulders and took a deep breath. "All right." I found my keys and fitted the right one into the lock.

The door opened and we went into the bookstore. All was dark. I flipped on the lights. The first area I checked was Frank's desk. The computer was gone, of course, and the ledger had been taken away. Frank's coffee cup was still there, half full of coffee, and it made my eyes fill up with tears. Nothing else looked any different than usual. Frank had not been much use at organizing books, but he wasn't a slob. Everything was neatly put away in drawers; nothing was on the floor. The lovely dark wood bookcases looked the same as they always did. I carefully avoided looking at the dark stain in the middle of the open area—there was nothing on the floor there, anyway.

"I don't see anything here," I said. "I could go shelf-by-shelf, I guess, but that would take hours."

"I don't think that will be necessary," said Todd. "It seems like the gunman had only about a minute to do whatever he did between the shot and leaving the scene. If you didn't hear him do anything around the shelves, it's unlikely he had any contact with them. Is there anything around the front entrance that is unusual?"

I looked. "No, nothing."

"All right, then. I think we can go now."

We walked to the back of the store and I turned out the lights before we went out. I locked the door again and Todd pulled on it to make sure it was secure.

"Well, that's over," I said gratefully.

"Yes. You did great. Really, great." His hand just rested on my shoulder briefly before he turned and led the way back toward the path.

"Can I go home now?"

"Of course. You must be sick of the sight of me."

"What I'm sick of is thinking about this murder."

"I know. I'm sorry you're so mixed up in it."

I shrugged. "At times like this the knowledge of the sovereignty of God is a great help. He has a reason for me to be going through this. I just have to trust Him. In fact, I just finished reading an old Puritan book called *All Things for Good*. This situation is probably God's idea of giving me a final exam on it."

"The one by Thomas Watson? Good book."

"You've read it?" I was incredulous.

"Yeah."

We walked silently for a few minutes. Then he said, "Do you really think God gives us final exams?"

"No, not really. I think that's the professor in me, always think in terms of tests and evidence of learning. Besides, God already knows how we are going to react to things. I think the tests are there so that *we* know where our hearts are at."

"I think you're right."

We had reached the parking lot by this time, and I pulled my car keys out of my pocket. "Well, I guess I'll see you tomorrow at three, huh? You must be pretty tired of seeing so much of *me*."

The smile appeared again. "I wouldn't say that, Miss Peters."

CHAPTER 6

I met Callie at the library the next day exactly at noon, and the librarian let us into the Special Collections room. It had been given that name in a burst of optimism with the hope that more rare books would be donated to the institution. As it was, there was only the one collection—the books willed to the college by Willard L. Jackson, whose portrait adorned the wall of the room with a plaque beside it to make sure everyone knew that *this* was the generous benefactor.

The prize of the collection, was, of course, the Bradstreet poem. It sat by itself in a glass case in the middle of the room, too valuable and fragile to risk handling by the general public. The other books were in a locked cabinet off to the side. The librarian unlocked it and got out the requested book: *Modern Chivalry, Volume One*, published in 1792. There had been six volumes altogether in the novel, brought out over a number of years, but the library only has the first. It is the most valuable, of course, and definitely a treasure for a small private school like this. Callie was allowed to sit at the antique desk in the room (also a bequest from Mr. Jackson) and read it.

While she did so, I took the opportunity to look at the Bradstreet poem again. It was beginning to be an old friend. The distinctive marks of water stains along one side only added to its charm. Sometime or other it had gotten damp, but it had survived. I admired, as I always did, the beautiful script, looking slightly cramped compared to the more fluid writing of the next century. Its angles and curves always reminded me of gothic architecture for some reason. The poem, though not my favorite of hers, was still beautiful, and a reminder that Christians through the centuries have had the same experience:

> By Night when Others Soundly Slept
> By night when others soundly slept
> And hath at once both ease and Rest,
> My waking eyes were open kept
> And so to lie I found it best.
> I sought him whom my Soul did Love,
> With tears I sought him earnestly.
> He bow'd his ear down from Above.
> In vain I did not seek or cry.
> My hungry Soul he fill'd with Good;
> He in his Bottle put my tears,
> My smarting wounds washt in his blood,
> And banisht thence my Doubts and fears.
> What to my Saviour shall I give
> Who freely hath done this for me?
> I'll serve him here whilst I shall live
> And Love him to Eternity.

I felt like I had had a moment of communion with Anne Bradstreet. "One Lord, one faith, one baptism…" in spite of the centuries separating us.

I gave a satisfied sigh and headed toward the opened cabinet. I hadn't really spent much time browsing through its contents. It was an eclectic mix. There were a couple valuable first editions, a few not-so-valuable first editions—mostly books few people have heard of, some manuscript volumes, and some books that were merely very old. One of these was the memoirs of a servant who had worked on George Washington's estate. I pulled it out and began to leaf through it.

The author, who had worked his way up from footman to butler, was probably a much better butler than he was a writer. To my knowledge, his reminiscences had never been reprinted, and I was not really surprised. However, it occurred to me that the book would contain some valuable information about the way servants were treated and their own feelings about their station. I wondered if it differed at all from the way people in service in Britain were treated and how they felt during the same time period. I decided to let Dr. Shaw in the History department know the book was in here, in case he hadn't seen it before. He had done a lot of work in the area of social history.

"I guess we should probably get going, huh?" Callie's voice pulled me out of the eighteenth century. I glanced at my watch.

"Ack! Only fifteen minutes till class! You're right, we ought to get going."

The librarian came back to ensure that the books were back in the right places, and to lock up the cabinet and the room after us, and Callie and I headed off to American Lit.

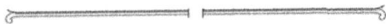

When class was over, I grabbed a sandwich from the grill on campus and then went to the police station. It was odd—I was almost starting to feel at home there. Some faces were now familiar, like the woman working at the desk out front who said she would tell Detective Mason I was there. I might have imagined it, but I thought she smiled at me more broadly than she would have if I were someone who had never been there before. I expected to be brought back to the interview room again, but instead Todd came out to where I was.

"Are you in a hurry?" he asked. "Do you have somewhere you need to be anytime soon?"

"Not really," I said. "I finished grading that stack of papers last night, so my calendar is pretty clear."

Idiot, I thought. *You might as well just scream "I have no social life!"*

"Mr. Delaney's cousin had an accident yesterday and broke his leg. He's in the hospital while they decide if they need to do surgery on it. I asked him if it would be all right if we talked to him at the hospital, and he agreed. It's in Tacoma, but that's not too far."

I consented, and nothing more of any importance was said until we were on the road. It's rather a pretty drive in spring—the road follows a river almost the whole way, and you can pretend you're out for a drive in the country.

"I have a question for you," Todd said. "When you saw that journal of Matthew Wilkes, could you read it?"

"Sure. It wasn't in code or anything, just ordinary writing."

"That's the problem; it isn't really ordinary writing. I mean, the letters are written differently, some of them, and he has some abbreviations for words that just seem odd. We've been trying to read it to see what Matt might have thought was valuable about it, but we are struggling. You didn't have the same problem?"

"No, it was fairly typical handwriting and abbreviations for the nineteenth century. But then I guess I've read a lot more of that than most people have."

"Exactly. I talked to the chief about hiring you as a consultant on this case. Right now it just means you would read the journal for us and see if you come up with anything important. But since you also knew the victim fairly well and have connections with a couple of suspects, it would be helpful to have your opinion as we sift through evidence."

"Sure," I said, thinking that "police consultant" would sound nice on my resume. "It wouldn't take me very long to read the journal. It's one of my few talents, actually: reading fast. Comes in handy for someone who makes a living out of reading. Well, and teaching. Teaching what I've read." I could feel myself beginning to babble. I made myself be quiet.

"Good," he said. "I'll see that you get the book when we get back to the station."

I nodded. "By the way, did you ever figure out what the note in the trash can meant about forgeries?"

He hesitated.

"Oh! I'm sorry. I'm sure you probably can't tell me that. I shouldn't have asked."

"Well, I suppose you are a consultant on the case, so I could tell you. We don't know yet. We thought that it might be written by the same person you heard Frank talking to on the phone, but we're not sure. The Office of College Development is headed by someone named Justin Marks—and his name obviously doesn't start with a K."

"Was Justin the one who called Frank?"

"He says he wasn't, although he admits that the college has approached Frank in the past about buying his building."

"Did he have any idea why someone would say the deed was forged?"

"We didn't ask him that. We don't always tell the

people we talk to everything we know."

"I see."

I looked out the window at the river. It was swollen with spring rains; the few ducks I could see were hurried along by the current. It reminded me of my life at the moment—since the murder, I felt like events had caught me up in a headlong rush toward the unknown, and I was like one of those ducks swimming frantically with startled expressions. Oh well. God was over all of it, untouched by the turbulence of the water. *As one who sits and gazes from above, Over the rivers to the bitter sea,* I thought. It was one of the poems we were going to discuss on Monday.

"It's funny how forgeries seem to be a recurring theme in my life right now," I said. "The book we're discussing at the book club on Monday also has a famous connection to forgeries."

"You go to a book club? You don't get enough reading done for your job?"

"Well, I started the book club, kind of as an outreach. It meets at the library, and it's called 'Reading the Classics.' A lot of old books touch on profound themes and a Christian worldview. I thought that even though I can't openly make it an evangelistic group, it might cause people to think about the deeper things in life. I also thought I could get to know people in Morris Creek that way."

"That's a great idea. What book are you discussing?"

"*Sonnets from the Portuguese*, by Elizabeth Barrett Browning. Usually we do novels, but someone asked if we could do poetry, so we're trying it out this time."

"Sounds intriguing."

I wondered if he was just saying that to be polite—most men do not find early nineteenth century woman poets to be anything but incomprehensible.

We found Frank's cousin John sitting up in bed with

71

his leg in a boot cast. He greeted us much more warmly than I would have thought a relative of Frank would.

"Sorry I couldn't make it in to the police station to see you today," he said. "I was trying to move a bookcase and it fell over on my foot. Entirely my own stupidity."

"Please don't worry about it," said Todd. "It was refreshing to be able to get out of the station this afternoon."

"And pleasant company too, I see," said John with a look I can only describe as teasing. I hate it when people do that—particularly people who don't even know you. I was dreading hearing Todd say the obvious rejoinder, either "we're just friends" or "we're just colleagues," or even "She's just working on this case with me as a consultant"—although that last one would be a bit of a mouthful.

Fortunately, Todd just ignored the comment, and pulled out a pen and a notebook.

"We wanted to ask you about your cousin Frank. We're very sorry for your loss."

"Thank you, but I haven't seen Frank in years. The real loss happened a good long time ago when he stopped speaking to me."

"We need to ask you if you know of any reason why someone would want to hurt Frank."

"No, but like I said, I haven't been in contact with him for years."

"Did you expect him to leave you anything in his will?"

"Heavens, no. That's the last think I would have expected. If anything, I thought he might leave something to Linda Johnson—she was his sweetheart years ago."

"Oh? Were they still in contact, do you know?"

"No idea. Unlikely, I'd say. She broke it off with him years ago—nearly twenty, at least. But I always thought he still had a soft spot for her."

"What happened?" I asked. Evidently this was the romantic secret behind Frank's embittered soul. A real-life male version of Miss Havisham.

"I don't know, exactly. She thought he had done something wrong, he told me. He'd done a lot for her, you know. She was the librarian at Wilkester College. It was on her account that he turned the hardware store into a bookstore. She said she wished there was a book dealer in Wilkester and he had inherited the store a few years before. He wasn't particularly excited about hardware, of course, and he thought he might as well switch to books. But like I said, afterwards she broke it off with him and she moved away not long after that."

"And he never told you what she thought he'd done?" asked Todd.

"I'm not even sure he knew for certain. But that's all he told me. After that he got cantankerous and quarrelsome—made enemies of pretty much everyone. He got mad at me for some reason—honestly, I can't even remember what it was."

"Like old John Harmon," I said without thinking.

"Who?" said Todd, turning to me with a pen poised over his notebook.

"Uh, From Dickens' *Our Mutual Friend*," I said sheepishly, vowing never to randomly allude to a book again. No point in reinforcing the nerd stereotype I already personified.

There wasn't much else John could tell us. The nurse came in with his dinner, so Todd thanked him for his information and we left.

On the way back to the police station, Todd asked me about how things had gone the other day when I went to help my friends with the foster kids. I regaled him with

73

tales about the amazing Cole family, and he told me about a policeman friend of his who also fostered kids. We swapped horror stories we had heard from the world of child services and then, feeling a little depressed, changed the topic to happy endings we'd heard of from the same system.

He gave me the diary when we got back to the station and told me to have a good weekend, and I went home to begin my work as an official police consultant.

Saturday morning was destined to be spent mostly on the phone. First I called my parents and my brother. I had texted them about the murder the day after it happened but hadn't really updated them on everything since. It took an hour for me to talk through all the details with them. I was glad I could discuss it without so much emotion. My family is one of the least dramatic clans I've ever met, and while I would not have been blamed for weeping on the phone with them, it made it much easier on all of us that I could converse about it sensibly.

The next phone call was to my friend Becky. She co-teaches the preschool Sunday School class with me, and I didn't want to have to cram a rapid explanation of the week's events between a lesson on Noah and snack time. I hadn't known Becky before we started teaching together a few months ago, but she was becoming a good friend. She was also single and about ten years younger than me. I was glad I called her. She was horrified by my experience and made me feel like I had coped with the whole thing admirably.

I had just hung up the phone with Becky and gotten ready to settle down with the diary when the phone rang. It was Kim.

"You've been holding out on me," she said.

"What?"

"You didn't tell me about Todd Mason."

"The detective? What was I supposed to tell you about him? I did tell you about him, remember? He's the guy in charge of the investigation."

"You didn't tell me he was interested in you."

"*What?*" I'm sure my voice rose by at least an octave. "He's not! At least, I don't think he is."

"Hmph. That's not what Ed says."

"Ed? When did he…oh, yeah, he told me he talked to Ed to clear me when I was a suspect. But he *had* to check up on me, you know."

"That's not what I mean. He called Ed this morning. Wanted to know if Ed could round up a couple people to help him clean the crime scene. He said he didn't want you to have to deal with it."

"Really? That's so nice of him. I was dreading that. But I was going to find some people to help me."

"He said he was afraid you wouldn't want to bother anyone about it and would just try doing it yourself."

"Oh, that's…" I was going to say ridiculous, but it came to me that I might very well have done that. "That's perceptive," I finished.

"He talked to Ed for at least fifteen minutes about you."

I could feel my face growing warm. "He seems like a very nice guy, but honestly, Kim, he might just be a bit of a flirt. I'm sure he knows he's good looking and successful… he's probably one of those guys who like women to be attracted to them and just flirt enough to give the woman some hope, but not enough to be accused of leading her on."

There was silence for a moment and then Kim added, "He wanted to know if you are seeing anyone."

"Oh."

"He also asked a lot of questions about the church and where you stand on certain doctrinal issues. I don't think he's just flirting."

"Oh," I said again.

"Well?" prompted Kim when I didn't say anything else. "Do you like him?"

I took a deep breath. "Well, yes. I haven't let myself think about it, because he *hasn't* said anything, but he seems like Our Kind of Person." That was our phrase for what Anne of Green Gables called a kindred spirit—someone who has the same outlook and knowledge base, who seems like someone you've known a long time.

"That's exactly what Ed said. Our Kind of Person. And I can't believe you didn't tell me about it."

"Like I said before, he hasn't said anything. You know my rule. I don't let myself imagine anything, let alone tell someone else, unless he says something."

She sighed impatiently. "I know. And it's a good rule. Usually. But just this once I think you ought to have told me."

"You're impossible, you know that?"

"I know. I won't bother you about it anymore. But if he does say something, you had better be on the phone to me within the next five minutes! And I'll have Ed do some checking on him. Don't want some shady character trying to woo our Katrina."

"I think I can safely say he's not wanted by the police," I said drily. "Now don't bring it up again. I'm having a hard enough time not thinking about it as it is!"

And if I had been struggling before, it was nothing to the battle after Kim's phone call. He wanted to know if I was seeing someone, did he? Ed and Kim approved of him already—that was unprecedented. He had organized getting my store cleaned up to save me from the stress of doing it myself. Every smile he'd given me was brought up for review in my mind. Every flattering thing he'd said, especially when he'd told me he wouldn't say he was tired of seeing me, was replayed.

I realized that I had been sitting with the diary in my lap, unread, for half an hour. I gave myself a firm shake, opened the book, and forced my mind to concentrate.

It was not a diary remarkable for its literary qualities. Matthew Wilkes recorded neither flora nor fauna, nor did he bother to explain his motives for anything he did. He was, however, rather obsessed with the weather. Every entry started with a statement about whether the day had been cloudy or sunny, if it had rained or snowed, and how hard the wind had blown. He was also a master of understatement. For example on June 14, 1848, the entry read, *Sun. Warm. No wind. This day m. Sarah Rochester of Port.* Imagine the man that spells out all the words relating to weather and then abbreviates "married" and "Portland"! I could, however, understand why the police were having a hard time figuring out what the journal said; between his abbreviations and his messy 19th century handwriting, it might very well have seemed like a secret code.

I read through all the entries for the first year of the diary. It faithfully chronicled the weather, of course, and sometimes what he ate (fish was a frequent meal). He was some kind of storekeeper, it seemed, and he gambled with "Roch" frequently. I figured out eventually that Roch was short for "Rochester," and was his brother-in-law. It didn't seem like he would win any husband of the year awards ("Sarah cross" showed up in the entries at least once a week), but I didn't see anything that the Wilkes family would be desperate to possess the book for.

Sunday morning was a welcome interlude of normalcy in my extremely tumultuous week. Word of my traumatic event had filtered through the congregation, and I got as many hugs as I could have wished for. The preschoolers were blissfully ignorant of murders and trauma and listened with rapt attention to Becky's lesson on Noah. Over the goldfish crackers and juice I made plans with Becky to go to her house for lunch after church. I had a feeling that if I went straight home I would spend the evening thinking about Todd and speculating about what he might be thinking—a singularly fruitless pastime.

Becky had inherited her grandmother's house. It was a charming little place with a yard that she was slowly transforming into an English country garden on the weekends—her weekdays being taken up with teaching third grade. We ate clam chowder and had cherry popsicles for dessert, a treat left over from the last visit of her young nephews. I volunteered to help her plant the trays of marigolds she had bought the previous day. She loaned me some sweats and garden gloves and we both got to work digging in the raised bed she had already spread with mulch.

"So you're helping the police now?" she asked. "Did they give you your own desk or anything?"

"No, nothing like that. I'm just reading through an old day-book—like a journal—and seeing if there's anything interesting in it that may pertain to the case. It was written by the man who founded the town."

"Matthew Wilkes?"

"Yeah, that's the guy. So far there's nothing very interesting in it."

"Well, I'll bet it gets more interesting when you get to the part where he saved people from the flood. They used to have a re-enactment every year. I think they only stopped because the guy who was the driving force behind it got sick, and no one else wanted to take it on. Besides, it was a sort of patriotic thing—being proud of your hometown and all that, and patriotism has gone out of fashion."

"Too true," I said, popping a partly-grown marigold out of its plastic pot and fitting it into the hole I had dug for it. "Although one of my students is a Matt Wilkes, and he seems to still have the old home-town spirit. He wrote a paper that mentioned that incident, but I didn't take care to memorize the details. I didn't know I would keep hearing about it."

"Oh, it's a marvellous story. The river, you know, goes right past the town. Matthew Wilkes had moved here from Seattle with his family to set up a general store—kind of an outpost in the wilderness. It's at the foot of the Cascade Mountains, and he thought trappers would appreciate something in the area. A few other families settled there, too, as they could do some farming and trapping and even logging, and send their goods down the river to Tacoma. The story goes that one night, after seeing smoke coming off one of the mountains, Matthew went out for a walk by the river and found that it was rising fast. People think now that it was a small eruption on Mount Rainier that melted a glacier, and the water gushed down the mountain into the river. He jumped on his horse and got a gun and rode around the settlement shooting into the air." Becky tossed aside the empty flower tray she had been using and looked around. "I thought I had another flat of flowers here."

"You do," I said. "It's over there."

"Ah, there it is. Thanks. Where was I?"

"Matthew shooting a gun into the air. Was that a signal?"

"Not exactly. People had been afraid of Native American attacks, so that woke them up and he shouted to them to get onto the boats and rafts they used to ferry their goods down the river. In ten minutes they had gotten themselves and what they could carry to the boats and rafts and were headed down the river. When they came back a few days later, everything had been washed away. I think only one person ended up dying—a guy who fell off one of the rafts. They rebuilt their homes, a little farther away from the river, and decided to call the town Wilkestown in his honor. He said he wanted it to be named for both him and his wife, and since her maiden name was Rochester, they came up with Wilkester."

"Oh yes! I said. "The name Rochester is in the diary. I have to say, so far the character in the journal seems very un-heroic—rounding up the neighbors in the middle of the night to save their lives isn't what I would have expected him to do. Perhaps he was one of those people that just ends up rising to the occasion."

"Yeah, sometimes you read about famous people who did something great in the second half of their lives, but when you look at their early life you'd never think they would have done that."

I finished with my tray of flowers and took off the gardening gloves. I wondered if that would be me: unremarkable for the first forty years of life and then had a missionary career where I did something astounding— although teaching at a mission school was unlikely to present an opportunity to be astonishingly heroic.

"I wonder if that will be me," I said. "Not the heroic bit, really, but just the second half of my life looking different than the first half."

"Oh really? Are you thinking about doing something different?"

"I've been thinking about it. I have a couple opportunities I'm considering. One idea is taking a teaching job in Papua New Guinea at a mission school."

"Whoa. That would be a life change, all right. Would you have to raise support and everything?"

"Yeah. Although I suppose I could sell the bookstore and use the proceeds to pay my own way."

"Well, that's an idea. What's the other possibility?"

"Foster care. I could keep doing editing and maybe teach just one class and then also foster one or two kids."

Becky finished putting the last of her plants in the ground. She sat upright on the grass and pulled off her gloves. "You know, I've wondered if I should be doing that. I teach school, and if the kids were school-aged, we'd be gone together and home together at the same time."

"That would be convenient," I said.

"And if we were both doing it we could babysit each other's kids if we needed a break or something."

I laughed. "I can just see us a year from now, exchanging ideas for birthday parties and clipping coupons for pop-tarts."

"Actually, I could see us doing just that," said Becky.

"That's what Kim said when she talked to me—that she could see me doing it. Well, maybe we should find out more about it. I'm sure there's some kind of informational meeting we could go to. I could ask Kim about it. No commitment, just looking into it."

"Good idea. Ask Kim." She heaved herself up off the lawn and offered me a hand to help me stand. "I think we deserve another popsicle."

We had our treat, and then I changed back into my own clothes and went home, eager to finish off reading the journal. I wondered what sort of laconic comment Matthew Wilkes might make about the tragedy. Something like "Skies clear, much wind. Town wiped out by a flood. Ate fish."

As it turned out, Matthew got much more verbose as the months and years went on. I read the entries about how the Wilkeses and "Roch" moved to Seattle, and then inland beyond Tacoma. It was made fairly clear that Mrs. Wilkes, who was now a mother, was eager to get her husband and brother away from the saloons and other unsavory spots in Seattle.

July 12, 1854 Storm in the eve. Sarah gives me no peace night or day about moving east. She says it is unwholesm. here for the child. I told her we would go if Roch comes. I am not lv. here to enjoy gd. life without me. Why do women cry so much?

I resisted the editor's impulse to add a question mark to the last sentence. The journal followed the travels and business establishment of the trio and I read about how a few other families settled nearby. Hour after hour I waded through the entries. Roch appeared to mature quite a bit as time went on; he was the one who fetched supplies from Tacoma every month, and Matthew frequently complained that he had not brought enough whisky.

Just when I had decided that I was getting too tired and would need to finish the journal the next day, I noticed that there was a gap of about a week in the journal, and the next entry was April 30, 1855. I could tell it was an important one: it was three times as long as anything Matthew had written before and had very few abbreviations. For once it did not start with a report on the weather.

Thurs last in the aft we saw smoke from the top of a mount and a noise like thunder. In the night Roch went out of the house because he could not sleep. He walked toward the river and soon saw by the full moon that the water was rising. He thought we would be in danger. He came and woke us. I did not believe him, being very tired but Sarah said we should make haste and go to the raft. She saw a river flood in Portl and many who were in boats were saved alive when others were swept away. She made a bundle of food and blankets and took the child and I followed her with my day-book and clothes. Roch said he wd. warn the others. He took my horse and my gun and I could hear him firing every few minutes. We got to the raft and saw that we were none too soon for the raft was almost loosed from its moorings. We waited for Roch. Other families came down the river on their boats, the Ferndales and the Smiths and the Poultens and others and at last Roch came back and said he had told them all. We untied the raft and went down the river swollen in the dark with the child crying all the while. It was almost dawn when Roch who had fallen asleep was pitched off the side of the raft having struck a rock and was not seen again. My wife cried and cried again and said we will see him no more.

I re-read it twice. I was sure I'd been told repeatedly that it was Matthew Wilkes who saved the community, but by the man's own account, it had been his brother-in-law who had been the hero. I looked at the clock—it was after midnight and I needed to go to bed. I could find out tomorrow how the wrong man got the credit for his act of bravery. One thing I could tell the police for sure: it was not a story the Wilkes family would have liked being known.

CHAPTER 7

I left a message for Todd the next morning, telling him I might have found something in the journal and asking him to call me back. He didn't, though, and I decided he must be pursuing some other lead, or even some other case. I dismissed it from my mind. Over and over again.

It was a very busy afternoon. I taught American Lit and then had to rush home and finish preparing for the book club that night. I try to be prepared well in advance for these meetings, but with the craziness of the week before, it hadn't happened.

I checked my email halfway through the preparation and found the editing job I had been expecting: a novel by an author who uses me frequently for her work.

"I decided to write a historical fiction novel this time," the email read. "Tell me what you think." I clicked on the document she had attached, curious about which time period the story was set in. Ancient times are actually easier to write as far as details go: so little is known about the dim past, and those who have studied it in depth are so few that you can make any number of mistakes without a single reader knowing the difference. On the other hand, Regency England buffs are legion and knowledgeable, and writers wade into those waters at their own risk. And the editor is supposed to catch the inaccuracies.

The first page of the novel made it clear that the story was set in colonial America. I heaved a little sigh and then told myself to be grateful for the work. And just maybe she had done her research well and there wouldn't be much to correct. I resolutely closed the document and went back to my preparation.

I arrived at the library right at 7:30, feeling a little flustered; I like to get there earlier than that. Most of the attendees were already there, about ten of them of various ages. I was just sorting through my notes and getting them arranged when there was that little bustling sound that happens when people murmur greetings and move their chairs around to make room for a new person in the group. I looked up and saw Todd. He grinned and gave a little wave. It was so unexpected that I just stared at him for a minute. I recovered what was left of my poise and thought rapidly. He must need to talk to me about the case or something. The other people were quietly chatting to each other, so as inconspicuously as I could I approached Todd who was maneuvering a chair into a gap in the circle.

"Did you get my message?" I said.

"This morning? Yes. Sorry I couldn't call you back— it was a hectic day. I thought maybe we could chat after the book club, if that's ok."

"Sure," I said. "You want to stay for the discussion?"

He grinned again. "That's why I came."

I glanced at the clock on the library wall and said, "We'd better get started."

The discussion began with people sharing their experiences of reading the poetry. Some had struggled with the language, others had rediscovered the beauty of verse. A couple of them had taken the opportunity to learn a little of Browning's biography, and there was some disagreement as to what her illness actually was.

"Before we start talking about which poems were your favorites," I said, "Did anyone have any questions about her life or her poetry in general?"

"I have one," said Todd. "I heard that this book had some connection to forgeries. Could you explain about that?"

I was tempted for a split second to say, "Where in the world did you hear that?" but sanity prevailed.

"It's quite a detective story," I said. "In the early 1930's two young men named Carter and Pollard who were in the rare book trade found out that they were both puzzled over the same thing. They kept running into first editions of nineteenth century books or pamphlets that were absolutely pristine, which is extremely rare for old books. Also, all of them had been discovered within the past thirty years or so, and they were all published just a year or two earlier than the versions everyone had thought were the first editions. One of the books was the book we read for this club, *Sonnets from the Portuguese,* only in this version it was just titled *Sonnets by E. B. B.* The young men were suspicious, as no one in the Brownings' circle had ever mentioned this first, small, private printing, which seemed very strange as all the other works Elizabeth had published were frequently mentioned.

"So the young men did something which had not really been done before: they analysed the paper and the type used in this volume. It turned out that the paper was made of chemical wood pulp, something that had not come into use until the 1880s. Also, the type was one of those that is called a kernless font, which was also not in use until the 1880s. Therefore, they knew that the book had not been published in 1847 as it claimed.

"Their researches into that one book applied to all

the pamphlets they were suspicious about, and they discovered that these so-called first editions shared something beyond anachronistic paper and sometimes anachronistic fonts: they had all been mentioned for the first time by the great bibliographer Thomas J. Wise. Does anyone know what a bibliographer is?"

My audience looked back at me blankly. It is a look I am used to encountering in students.

"A bibliographer," I went on, "Is someone who compiles a list of every single thing an author ever published, including each edition and printing. It may sound like boring stuff, but students of literature use these exhaustive bibliographies all the time as they research particular authors. It is also a guide for people in the rare book trade to help them know what is valuable. Wise was an extremely knowledgeable man and really the highest authority in England for that sort of thing.

"At first they thought Wise had been duped into recognizing these books as valid first editions. After all, he was very, very vocal about how evil forgers were. But the evidence mounted up against him, and they discovered that in the late nineteenth century he had had access to a printer's store. That store, they found out, contained every single one of the fonts used in those first editions. He had printed off many copies of the pamphlets and then held on to them for years, slipping references to them in his bibliographies and then telling collectors he would keep an eye out on their behalf to see if one could be purchased.

"When it all came out, he was discredited, of course, and the world of book collectors was shaken to its core. But it started an era of more scientific investigation into forgeries which has continued ever since."

I stopped to take a breath. "Well, that's probably more than you wanted to know, but that's the connection between Elizabeth Barrett Browning and the world of forgeries. Now, who would like to share a poem they particularly liked?"

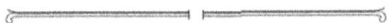

The group disbanded at 8:30, and Todd helped me and the librarian put the chairs back where they belonged at the study desks.

"Do you want to grab a cup of coffee or a piece of pie?" he asked. "Sally's is open late."

We sat in a booth at Sally's and ordered chocolate cream pie and decaf coffee.

"Now I know I'm getting old," I said. "I used to be able to drink regular coffee at any time and still get to sleep at night."

"Yeah, those were the days," said Todd. "I remember when it seemed exciting to stay up all night. Now it's one of the things I dislike most about the job."

"Does that happen often?"

"No, thankfully."

The coffee arrived with the pie, and I stirred sugar and cream into my cup.

"So, what did you think of the book club?"

"I thought it was great. Everyone seemed to really enjoy it."

"Yes, I was quite relieved, especially since we don't do much poetry. It takes a lot more concentration to read old poems than it does novels—even old novels. But they coped very well."

Todd took a bit of his pie. "Mmm, that's good. I thought it was interesting that no one commented on my favorite of the sonnets."

"You have a favorite sonnet?" I expected him to be

joking and waited for the punchline.

"Yeah. It's the one that starts off, 'If thou must love me, let it be for nought except for love's sake only.'"

"Sonnet Fourteen," I said. "Did you study it for school or something?"

"No, no, I found it when I was reading the book this weekend. In preparation for the group."

"You read all those sonnets this weekend just for the club?"

He nodded.

"But you didn't say anything about it when we were discussing them."

"Well, I was new. And I didn't want to look like I was trying to be teacher's pet."

"You needn't have worried. Nobody who isn't anxious about their grade tries to get on my good side. But why did you ask the question about forgeries?"

"I was interested. This case might have to do with a forged deed, and it's something I know very little about. The FBI deals with forgeries all the time, but the local police force not so much."

"You'd better ask Professor Weatherill about it. He knows way more than I do."

"I did talk to him, actually, about the email Frank sent him regarding a forgery. He said that he hadn't gotten around to answering the email, but he would have told him that he should take it straight to the police."

"If he'd done so, what would the police have done about it?"

Todd laughed. "Probably contacted someone like Weatherill to see if the document was genuine."

"And can you get the deed so it can be analysed?"

"The wheels are in motion for that, but it will take another day or so. We believe it's at Frank's house, but we haven't finished going through all the papers there."

"I see." I took another bite of the pie. It really was good.

"And now perhaps you can tell me what you found in that journal."

"Oh! I'd almost forgotten about that. Well, have you heard the story of the founding of the town?"

"I think so. With the flooding and the middle of the night escape?"

"Right. I've had the story told to me three times, and each time it was said that Matthew Wilkes was the one who roused the settlers and got them to their boats. In the journal, though, it was his brother-in-law, Rochester, who did that. And Rochester died that night, falling off the boat."

"Well, well," said Todd, leaning back in his seat and putting his fork down on the empty plate. "You're right, that isn't something the family would want known."

"Is it worth killing over, though?" I said.

"It might be. The Wilkes family get a lot of perks for having that man as an ancestor. I don't know if all that would go away if he wasn't the hero he was painted, but they'd certainly feel somewhat disgraced. It's possible they would lose school scholarships, which would be a financial blow."

"That's what I was wondering. I haven't had time yet today to keep reading and find out why Matthew got the credit, but it's probably in there."

"Well, what you've told me is reason enough to bring Matt in for questioning. We'll do that tomorrow."

I looked at my watch. "I'd better get going, actually. I have a class in the morning and one tomorrow night, plus I need to finish reading this journal and get to work editing a novel for someone."

"Yes, and I have a couple people to interview tomorrow. We'll talk to Matt and we've also located Linda Johnson—the former sweetheart of Frank. I need to talk to her as well. I'll take care of that," he said as I looked at the bill and dug in my purse for my wallet. "Official police business chats mean coffee and pie are provided free of charge."

"Thanks," I said. "I'll let you know when I've finished the journal, and if there's anything else that seems important."

"Great. Let me walk you to your car."

I opened my mouth to tell him he didn't need to and then shut it. It was late, it was dark, and to refuse a police escort for a reason like "I don't want to bother you" would just seem rude.

In other circumstances the walk across the parking lot might have seemed romantic. There was a full moon and a gentle breeze and we were walking closely enough together that we could have held hands. We didn't, of course, and I was impatient with myself for even thinking of it. He was a law officer and I was a consultant and he was being protective from habit. That was all.

No sooner had I determined this than he said, "I wish our every interaction was not so completely professional."

I unlocked my car door and opened it. "I didn't think it was," I said. "I mean, we've talked about faith and foster care and other things. It hasn't all been police business." I got into the car and reached for the seat belt.

He stood there looking down at me with that half smile of his. "That wasn't quite what I had in mind," he said.

I must have looked taken aback, because he gave what I can only call a rueful laugh and said, "Goodnight." He shut the door gently and waited there while I started the car, gave a little wave, and drove away.

I hardly had time to eat the next day. Matt was missing from English Comp in the morning, and I wondered if it was because he was at the police station answering questions. Or being arrested. When class was over I drove home to get as much done as I could before my evening class.

First things first: I speed-read through the rest of the journal and discovered that when the Wilkeses returned to the area after the flood, they found that the other settlers had recognized the horse but not the rider during the middle-of-the-night ordeal. Furthermore, it was known that Rochester did not own a gun, so the families that had been warned simply assumed that Matthew had been their savior. Mrs. Wilkes had wanted to set the record straight, but Matthew persuaded her that their store would benefit from the good press (my words, not his). The "ester" part of "Wilkester" was put in to honor the late brother of Mrs. Wilkes, although the other settlers seemed to have thought it was only to mark his passing as the one life lost in the ordeal. They did not know it was to him they owed their lives.

While this discovery was fascinating and threw an even less-flattering light on Matthew Wilkes, I didn't think it would make any real difference to the case. I thought about calling Todd to tell him, but then decided that if I delayed a bit before I called, it would give him time to finish interviewing people first. I wanted to find out what they had said.

The next order of business was to start editing the novel I'd been sent. Sheila Farnell is a good writer—rarely do I have to correct her punctuation or fix a non-parallel construction. Moreover, she has interesting plots that keep my attention. Nothing is worse than trying to edit a book that is so boring you find your mind wandering to other things even while you read. In my early days of editing, when I took any job I could get, I was sent the draft of a book that extolled the glories of mathematics. You can imagine my difficulty. I kept myself alert—that is to say, conscious—by writing things like "Haha!" or "You can't be serious!" in the space for review notes. And then I deleted all my sarcastic comments before sending it back to the author. One does what one must to get through it.

As I read the first chapter of Sheila's book, I could tell that she had done some research about the time period, which was a relief. However, the problem with writing historical fiction is that you don't know what you don't know. It's easy to make assumptions without realizing it. The first problem showed up in the fourth paragraph. The heroine was at a ball, dancing a waltz. So far, so good, but what Sheila didn't know was that what she was describing—a man and woman moving together with his arm around her waist and their other hands clasped—was not what was meant by waltz in 1770. I wrote a note in the margin to that effect.

The next item was the heroine drinking a glass of orange juice at breakfast. I suggested that chocolate (what we call hot chocolate) or tea would have been a more likely drink. Beer would also have been more likely than juice, but I didn't want to suggest that. A heroine who was chugging down alcoholic beverages at her morning meal would affront the sensibilities of most readers of Christian romance novels, and trying to present it in such a way that readers would understand it to be period-appropriate would render the narrative clumsy and distracting. Best to stick to tea.

I worked on the novel until almost time to leave for class. Then I reheated some leftover spaghetti, ate it as quickly as I could (my mother would have said I wolfed it down, but that's such an unflattering image, isn't it?), and left for the college.

This was the class I had let out early the previous week. We had a lot to cover, and I whisked the students through my lecture on different ways of arranging information in an argumentative paper at breakneck speed. It was no wonder that a couple of students wanted to talk to me afterwards to clarify just what I had said; several of them were not native English speakers and were understandably confused. By the time I finished talking to the last student, the rest of the class had disappeared.

It was pretty late when I shut the door of the classroom—it must have been about 9:45. Wilkester is hardly the crime capital of the country (despite the occasional murder), but I was always a little nervous going to the faculty parking lot alone. It's not terribly well-lit at night, and there is a row of bushes beside the path that makes me nervous. I always try my best to walk with a group of students as far as I can, and then when we part ways I make a dash for my car, keys in hand. Actually, "dash" is overstating it, but I try to move more quickly.

The student I had been talking to got onto his bicycle not far from the classroom building and I had to walk alone farther than usual. I walked as briskly as I could, humming a little tune. It's not at all unusual to have a few people walking around campus at that time, and at first I didn't particularly notice the footsteps behind me. When I did notice them, they were a good ways behind me—far enough that they weren't a concern. As I kept listening, though, they seemed to be coming closer.

Silly, I told myself. *You're being paranoid.* All the same, I wished I had followed through in getting some pepper spray to keep in my purse when Kim had suggested it. It flashed through my mind that it could be the killer. And if so, pepper spray would do nothing to protect me from a gun.

After a moment or two there was no doubt about it—the footsteps *were* closer. I made a hasty plan. I would get my phone out and dial 911, but not hit send. Then I would turn around and see who it was. If it was someone that was in any way threatening, I would hit send. Then I could shout out a description of the person, and if they shot me … well, then the police would have an exact time of death recorded and a description of the killer.

Quickly I slid my hand into my coat pocket and pulled out my phone. Since one hand was holding my attaché case, I had to try to unlock the screen and dial the number one-handed. I don't know if it was because I was starting to tremble or because I am naturally clumsy, but there was a fumble, and I dropped the phone. Involuntarily, I cried out.

"Hey, Katrina, you ok?" said a voice.

I spun around and saw Todd. I felt light-headed with relief. I also could have happily punched him. He jogged the last few steps up to me and bent down to pick up my phone.

"Sorry, did I scare you?"

"Just a little," I said, hoping that it didn't qualify as a lie. It was the first time I'd seen Todd not wearing a suit—he was in jeans and a sweater tonight. He was carrying a briefcase, though. "I really wasn't expecting to see you. How did you find me?"

"You gave us your schedule, remember?"

"Oh…right. I'd forgotten."

"Do you always walk out here alone at night after class?"

"Not on purpose. I try to walk with the students as much as I can."

"We'll have to see what can be done to make this safer. It's not good." His eyes scanned the area, taking in the bushes, the dim lighting, and the secluded location.

It's not personal, I reminded myself. *He'd be concerned over the safety of any female in this situation.*

"Did you need something? I mean, as happy as I am to have an armed escort to my car…"

He chuckled. "Yeah, I wanted to bring you up to speed on the case. Do you want to talk in your office?"

I sighed. "I wish we could. But adjunct professors don't have offices. We could talk in my car if you want."

"I suppose that would work."

I unlocked the car and hoped I hadn't left any trash on the passenger side floor. I usually remember to take stuff out and throw it away, but I wouldn't be shocked if there was something there. At least it was dark.

"I was wondering how all your interviews went," I said after we had gotten in and closed the doors. There was enough light to see Todd's face dimly. "I especially wondered about Matt. He wasn't in class this morning."

"No, he wouldn't be. We brought him in for questioning. He admitted to wanting the book and knowing what was in it. When he found the journal at the store, he searched for entries around the date of the flood and found the one you told me about."

"Did he admit to trying to break into the store?"

"Yep. Says he panicked and thought he would lose his scholarship if the truth were made public. He also seemed to genuinely believe that the journal is family property. But he denied doing the murder."

"Do you believe him?"

"He does have an alibi. At the time of the shooting he was with a relative who confirms that. He doesn't seem to be the killer."

"Oh, I'm glad," I said. "So glad. I hated the thought that I might have had a murderer for a student, you know?"

"Yeah, I know."

"And did you talk to the other lady, too? Frank's old sweetheart?"

"I did. Linda Johnson says she broke things off with Frank because she was informed that Frank's family had gotten the store illegally. She was told that fraud was a family characteristic, and that they were all in on it. She thought it would be best to distance herself from a such a corrupt family. I got the impression that the attraction was much stronger on Frank's side than on hers."

"And was it true? About the store being gotten illegally?"

"I don't know. The person had told her a story about the grandfather causing an accident that killed the former owner and then forging the deed to the property. She said it sounded plausible at the time."

"Did she mean she doesn't believe it anymore?" I traced the circle of the steering wheel with my finger. If Frank hadn't really owned the store, then did I really own it now? Not that I wanted the store, of course, but if selling it would fund a missionary venture...

"She doesn't know if she believes it or not. The person who told her seemed a credible source, although she now thinks that it was possibly made up to get her away from Frank."

"Who was it?"

"John's brother. Frank's cousin. She came to suspect later that he had an unrequited attachment to her. He is now deceased."

I sighed. "So there's no one to check her story with."

"Well, I did call John and talk to him again. He says his older brother did like Linda and didn't like Frank. He said he wouldn't put it past his brother to make up such a story and feed it to Linda."

"So you think it wasn't true at all?"

"Not necessarily. John said the Delaneys weren't exactly a byword for honesty in the community. He's not a Delaney, you know—he was related to Frank from the mother's side and had very little reason to either believe or disbelieve the story."

"Linda must have told someone what she heard."

"She did. Her family. And now her nephew works at the college. You want to guess what his name is?"

"Does it start with a K?"

"Yep. Kevin Schmidt. Vice President for Finance."

"Ohhh."

"Know anything about him?"

"No, just his name."

"We're checking into him. We'll probably pull him in for questioning tomorrow."

"Well, that was a good day's work, huh? You found out a lot of things today that you didn't know before."

"True. And there was something else I wanted to talk to you about." He'd been looking out the front window, but now he faced me.

"Oh?" my heart skipped a beat.

He opened his briefcase and pulled out a folded piece of paper.

"This," he said, handing it to me. I was glad it was dark; I would have hated if he saw me look disappointed.

"What is it?"

"It's the deed to Frank's store. We found it."

"Oh!" I unfolded it but it was too dark to read it. I switched on the car's overhead light.

"Does it look genuine to you?" asked Todd. "It looks written by a typewriter—that seems a little modern for the date, doesn't it?"

I looked at the date: 1894.

"No," I said, "As far as I know, typewritten documents were standard by the 1890's. The paper feels right for the era, too. But I'm not an expert—you really need to send it to a lab to make sure." I handed it back to him.

"Thanks," he said. "That's very helpful. I think that's everything I needed to tell you."

"I can't believe you came all the way here to find me this late at night just to get me up to speed."

"I didn't. I mean, we were nearby, at the bookstore. When we finished I thought you might be coming out of class and I thought I'd see if I could catch you. Oh, wait!" Todd went back into his briefcase and pulled out a key.

"What's this?"

"Frank's key to the store. The police no longer need it, and I thought I'd give it to you. The carpet is cleaned, by the way."

"You cleaned it?"

"Along with your friend Ed. He's a really good guy."

"Yeah, I know. Thanks. Really, thanks. I appreciate it so much!"

"No problem." He fiddled with the handle of his briefcase. "It was my pleasure." He cleared his throat. "I—" His phone rang. "Excuse me," he said to me, getting out of the car and closing the door behind him.

"Detective Mason," I heard him say. Then there were a lot of *uh-huh's* and *no's* and a *yes*. Then I heard, "I'd better come now... Yeah, I'll be there as soon as I can. Bye."

He opened the door of my car and reached in for the briefcase.

"I've got to go—something came up with another case. I'll talk to you soon."

"Ok," I said. My "goodbye" was lost in the sound of the door shutting.

CHAPTER 8

That was the last I heard from Todd for almost a week. I toyed with the idea of calling him to see what Kevin Schmidt had said or find out if the lab had analyzed the property deed but decided against it. If Kevin had been arrested for murder, I was sure I would have heard about it. Todd probably had his mind on this other case now and didn't need me distracting him with unnecessary questions. And there was always the chance he would think I was pursuing him, and I wasn't. Was I? Would I have thought about calling up the detective in charge of the case if he had been an unattractive married man? I wasn't sure.

On Friday the Coles invited me to eat dinner with them and go see Josh play a basketball game. I accepted with pleasure. I hadn't been to one of Josh's games in a while, and it would give me a chance to hang out with my favorite kids.

Things didn't quite go according to plan, though. This time it was Mia who had a meltdown right before we were supposed to leave for the game. I volunteered to stay home with her so the others could go, but it was decided that Kim would stay, too.

"To be honest," she told me after Mia's hour-long tantrum subsided, "I'm glad I could stay home and talk to you. It's been a crazy week and I'm tired. Plus, we need to spend some time catching up."

"I agree," I said plopping down on the couch next to her. "How has your week been?"

She waved away my question with her hand. "Not me, silly, you! What's new with *you*?"

"Not much," I said. "I still don't officially own the bookstore, the murder is still unsolved, there's still a month left before the end of the semester…oh! But I am editing a new novel."

Kim threw a pillow at me. "That's not what I meant, and you know it. What's new with the detective?"

"Not a thing."

"You mean he *still* hasn't said anything?"

I shook my head.

"But—but he cleaned your carpet with Ed on Tuesday."

"He did, and it was extremely kind of him, but he still didn't say anything."

"Well, that stinks," said Kim. "And it puzzles me. Ed was sure he was serious."

"There was a moment the other night when I thought he might have been going to say something, but he had a phone call right then and had to rush off."

"There, you see? He *is* interested."

I held up a hand. "Not so fast. For one thing, I have no idea what he was going to say. For another, I haven't heard from him in days. I don't like guys that throw out hints and then don't follow through. If he wants to pursue me, he should just do it—no hesitating and tiptoeing around the idea. If he isn't sure yet if he likes me or not then he should stop doing things that make me wonder. You know?"

Kim sighed. "I know. He didn't seem like that kind of guy to Ed, but maybe he is." She twirled her hair broodingly for a minute. "Oh well. Nothing to be done about that now, I guess. Have you thought about what you're going to do with the bookstore?"

"No. In the last couple days I've started using it as my office, though—I can study and do lesson planning and paper-grading there. It's quiet and very close to campus. Much easier than driving home and back to campus again."

"I'm guessing you're not open for business."

"No. For one thing it's not legally mine yet, and with this whole deed thing hanging over my head I don't feel like I can make any real decisions. Besides, I can't run a store and teach at the same time."

"No, I suppose not. You know what I was thinking? It would be a great ministry hangout place for students. You know, like a Christian bookstore that was also a coffee store, where there could be talks on different topics or music nights."

"That's a thought," I said. "I've heard about places like that. It would be neat. But I don't want to run it."

"It might be something our church would like to get involved in."

"You think? That would be great. But again, it's not legally mine yet. I can't make any decisions now. And if I decide to go to the mission field, selling the place would be the most logical move."

"Still thinking about that, huh?"

"Yes. And Becky and I were wondering if there's some kind of informational meeting she and I could go to about foster care. We're both thinking about it."

"Ooo!" Kim squealed, "That would be great!"

"*Thinking* about it," I said firmly. "No decisions made."

"Understood," said Kim. "I'll find out when the next meeting is. Ok, you want to help me whip up some brownies for the family when they get home?"

"Sure. Is Mia settled enough to help us?"

"I don't know. I'll peek into her room and see how she's doing."

While Kim went to check on Mia, I looked at some of Deirdre's artwork that was lying on a side table.

"Deirdre's getting really good," I said to Kim when she returned.

"I know, isn't she? She's trying to pick out which picture she should submit for the showcase gallery that's coming up for her art class. Mia's asleep, so I think I'll just leave her alone."

"Sounds good," I said. "That means I get to lick the bowl all by myself."

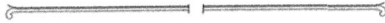

My phone rang Monday right after my class. It was Todd, wanting to know if I could come to the station to discuss new developments in the case.

"I'll be right there," I said. I didn't like to admit that I suddenly felt like it was beautiful day.

The room we sat in this time had a window, some comfortable chairs, and a potted plant, almost like a small living room. It made a nice change from the interrogation room we'd been in a few times.

"How was your weekend?" Todd asked.

"Quiet," I said. "I graded papers and did some editing. On Sunday I went up to my favorite spot in the mountains. The weather's warmed up so much now that it was a lovely day."

"You like to go hiking?"

"I like a leisurely stroll through the forest. I don't really do mountain climbing."

"Do you like camping?"

"Yeah, I like that, too." The look of interest in his eyes was flattering but I was wary now. If he was trying to charm me into falling for him to boost his own ego or whatever, it wasn't going to work.

"I thought you had something to tell me about the case," I said.

"Right, right. Sorry. I thought you'd like to know about Kevin Schmidt."

"Yes, I would. What happened?"

"Turns out his job is on the line. The college is not in the best of shape financially, and a lot of it has to do with decisions Kevin made. He thought he might get back into the good graces of the powers-that-be if he was able to arrange the sale of the bookstore to the college."

"Did he believe the story about the forged deed?"

"Oh yes. Completely. He thought it would give him leverage over Frank."

"It's hard to believe he would admit to trying to blackmail Frank. That's a crime, isn't it?"

"Well, I think he was anxious to avoid being charged with murder. Besides, he admitted it without really meaning to do so. Interrogation is an art form. You get good at getting the information you need without the person realizing what they are letting out."

"And will he get in trouble for blackmail now?"

"It would be hard to prosecute him for it. For one thing, it didn't work."

"Would he have reason to murder Frank?"

"Not unless he thought whoever would own the store after Frank would be willing to sell. And even then...I don't know if he was that desperate to keep his job, or even if he was positive that getting that building for the college would be enough to impress his superiors."

"Does he have an alibi?"

"No. He says he was in his office alone during the fatal hour. He might have been. No one remembers him being there or not. He could easily have left his office, gone over to the store, shot Frank, and come back to the office. It's unlikely anyone would remember seeing him out and about at that time. What's more, he has a gun registered to him that he claims was stolen a month ago."

"And can you tell if it was?"

"Well, he certainly filed a report on a stolen gun a month ago. But then if he were planning to use it to commit murder, he might claim it was stolen, use it, and then dispose of it afterwards."

"So will you arrest him?"

"There's not enough evidence against him. His motive is very weak and there's nothing to tie him to the murder."

"Will it matter if the property deed is proven to be a forgery?"

"It isn't. We got word back from the lab this morning. There's an almost undetectable watermark in the paper from the land company—almost impossible to reproduce. The deed is definitely genuine. It looks as if John's brother fabricated the entire tale."

"And Frank knew it wasn't true," I concluded. "That's why he wasn't intimidated. I remember hearing him say, 'That's an empty threat.' That must have been what he was referring to."

"Most likely," agreed Todd.

"Any other leads, then?"

"I'm afraid not. There's always the possibility that someone will come forward with something new."

"And if they don't? Will it be a cold case?"

"Eventually, if there are no more leads it will become

a cold case, yes."

"Poor Frank," I murmured. "It seems like someone should be held accountable."

"They will. Hopefully in this world in the not-too-distant future, but assuredly in the next world."

I nodded. "I know." I could feel my eyes filling with tears.

"I'm not going to give up, Katrina," said Todd, leaning forward. "If it takes weeks or months, I'm going to keep trying."

"'Neither snow nor rain nor heat nor gloom of night' will keep you from your duty, huh?" I said, trying for a lighter note. "Except of course that you're not a postal worker, and that's not even an official slogan for the post office." Todd wrinkled his forehead. "I don't like misattributed quotes," I explained.

Todd looked at me intently for another minute and then said, "Can I ask you a question? Why are you just an adjunct professor? You are extremely knowledgeable, you have wide experience, and I've seen you teach—you make the subject come alive. You ought to be a professor at a top university."

I laughed a little. "Well, that was the plan. It's a long story."

"I like long stories."

"Well then." I cleared my throat. "Once upon a time I was on the tenure track at UCSC. I don't know if you know how that works."

Todd shook his head.

"You become an assistant professor for six years. I mean, you do everything a full professor does, but your title is 'assistant professor.' Unless you are dismissed for gross negligence or an inability to teach during that time, you get tenure and become a full professor. Especially if you've published something in the meantime."

"So what happened?"

"The head of the English department objected to my beliefs about feminism, among other things. That is, she was extremely feminist and I'm...not."

"You were accused of teaching your own viewpoint? What about academic freedom?"

"No, they couldn't accuse me of foisting my 'backward' beliefs on the students—although they tried. It was really more of my personal convictions they didn't like. Convictions that came out in my conversations with colleagues and my affiliations with things like a campus Bible study. It was all painted to look like I was just not needed in the English department there; after all, my published book was on the influence of George Herbert on Anne Bradstreet, which was much too religious an idea for that department to think important. They didn't have to fire me. You're automatically let go if you don't get tenure."

"But why didn't you get a job at another college? As a full professor, I mean."

"If you've been turned down for tenure at one college, it's almost impossible to be hired as a full professor at another school. It's just the way things work. And with the state of most college budgets, they'd rather hire a bunch of adjunct faculty to teach the bulk of the classes— especially lower-division courses. They don't have to pay medical or dental or retirement for adjuncts, they can drop them at will if they want to, and they don't have to pay them very much."

"So you came here to be an adjunct professor."

"Yeah. I'd known Ed and Kim in college and kept in touch with them when Ed came to work at Wilkester. When they had a need for an adjunct, he told me I should come. I actually beat out a couple other people for the job, probably because I'd done work on Bradstreet and they have a manuscript of hers here. But it's been a good job in a lot of ways. The cost of living is cheaper here than Southern California, so I can live on what I make at the college along with some freelance editing work. And I love my church and I have friends…" I almost started to tell him about my desire to do more with my life, but something held me back.

"That's rough," he said. "Not about the church and your friends, but the whole professorship thing. I'm sorry that happened to you."

"Well, in a way it was suffering for my faith. I know if I had changed my views I would have gotten tenure. The apostles thought it was a privilege to suffer for their faith, and I've tried my best to make that my attitude as well."

"You remind me of some men I met in India when I was traveling around and visiting different ministries. These guys lived in an area of militant Hinduism. They had actually been beaten for their faith and their houses were burned down. One man had lost an arm from the beating. What struck me was their gratitude for being counted worthy to suffer. Of course it was illegal for them to be harassed like that, but the authorities did nothing to help them or stop the persecution. But instead of being angry that their rights were violated, they were praising God for strengthening them to endure persecution."

"Wow. My suffering is piddly compared to theirs. It must have been a fascinating trip—I'd love to go there. Did you go by yourself?

There was a pause.

"No. Uh, no. With my wife."

I just stared at him. *His wife?*

"My ex-wife."

"Oh." I couldn't think of another thing to say. My

heart sank. Literally. I felt it descend from my chest to my stomach. An x-ray would have proved it, I'm sure.

"I've got something to give you," he said rather abruptly. He was gone and back in less than two minutes, carrying a small stack of books.

"These were at Frank's house," he said. "The house was willed to 'any living relatives to divide as they wish,' so it goes to John as the only living relative. He went through the house with us the other day to see if there might be anything that would pertain to the case besides the things we'd already gotten, and he saw these books. He said they rightly belonged to the bookstore, and he didn't want them in any case, so I'm giving them to you."

I took the stack from Todd.

"Thanks," I said, glancing at the covers. "They look pretty old—probably valuable." I stood up. "I'd better get going, if there's nothing else. I have a book to finish editing, along with—well, other stuff." I clutched my stack of books and smiled—probably mechanically, but it was all I could manage at the moment.

"Yeah, that's all," said Todd. "Thanks for coming in. 'Bye, Katrina."

He did not offer to walk me to my car.

I drove home in that stunned state where you later can't remember anything about the journey. I felt somehow betrayed. Todd had presented himself as Our Kind of Person, and he wasn't. Not really. If I asked him about his divorce he would probably tell me, "we just grew apart." Our Kind of Person doesn't think that way about marriage. For us, marriage is for life, even if you fall out of love with your spouse.

But there is such a thing as a biblical divorce, said my conscience, and I had to concede that. I didn't believe that every divorce was sinful. But I knew that if I married a divorced person I would feel cheated out of having a soulmate. Kim's taunt came back to my mind: "Still waiting for Captain Wentworth, eh? … 'I have loved none but you…'"

"Yes, I am," I said aloud. "There's *nothing* wrong with wanting that. I don't have to marry anyone if they aren't what I'm looking for."

Deirdre's words broke into my memory: "What if *God* wants you to marry him?"

"He doesn't," I muttered stubbornly. "He doesn't! And it doesn't matter anyway. I doubt he was really interested in me, and now that the case has gone cold I probably won't be seeing him again. It's a good thing."

I pulled into my parking space, put my head down on the steering wheel, and sobbed.

CHAPTER 9

The rest of that week seemed very flat. I blamed it on all kinds of things, but I knew I was just mourning the loss of a possibility. I had tried not to let myself hope, but I had hoped in spite of myself, and now I had to pay the price for it. I wondered if perhaps the best thing to do was go to Papua New Guinea and leave it all behind me. I was going to have to decide soon. Their school year started in September and I'd have to let them know by June, less than two months away.

On Friday afternoon I sat in the bookstore and edited the final few chapters of Sheila's novel. The climax of the book involved a scene between the heroine, the young and beautiful Albina, daughter of the largest landowner in Virginia, and her love interest, the dashing but penniless footman Edward on a neighboring estate.

All through my edits of the book I had debated whether I should inform her that such an unequal marriage might *just* have been within the realm of possibility, but no one around the lovestruck couple would have viewed the match as anything but completely appalling. I had decided against making a note of it; for me to suggest that she change the social status of the hero to make it more period-accurate would be to imply that she re-write most of the novel, as his servanthood was a major part of the plot.

However, I did feel I must enlighten her that if someone were to knock on the door of a colonial mansion in the middle of the night, it would be a servant who came to answer it and not the daughter of the house wearing her nightgown, even if she *had* been rummaging in the kitchen for a late-night snack (also very unlikely).

However, I would not at all be surprised if Sheila chose to keep that scene anyway. It was very romantic with the moonlight shining on Albina's long dark hair, at last let down from its usual elaborate arrangement, and the hero Edward gently touching her face, brushing away the tear that had come when he had announced that he loved her too much to ask her to share the frontier life he was leaving to pursue.

I was doing my utmost to keep myself from imagining what it would feel like to be the woman who was the object of such tender consideration and caresses, when my phone rang.

"Hi, Aunt Katrina? It's Deirdre."

"Hey, Deirdre, what's going on?"

"I was wondering if you would be free tomorrow to pick me up from my friend's house. She's having a birthday party—just a few girls and we're going to give each other makeovers. My parents can drop me off, but then they have this planning meeting for the foster families' Fun Day and Josh has to watch Ben and Mia."

"Sure, sweetie, I'd love to. What time?"

"It's supposed to be finished at seven-thirty. I can text you the address."

"No problem. See you tomorrow."

"Thanks, Aunt Katrina! And mom wants to talk to you."

I could hear her handing the phone over to Kim.

"Hi, Katrina. Just wanted to tell you that there's an

informational meeting next Saturday afternoon for potential foster carers, if you want to tell Becky. I don't remember the time, but I'll find out and let you know. They're having the meeting at that big Methodist church on 8th Street."

"Oh, great, thanks! I'm sure we'll be there."

I sent a quick text to Becky and then made myself concentrate to finish up editing the last bit of the book. When it was done, I emailed it back to Sheila for her first pass at revising it. I got up to stretch and wandered through the bookstore. It still didn't feel like mine. I supposed that was because I wasn't intending to keep it and run it as a bookstore—either I would sell it and all the books, or I would sell most of the books and use it as a ministry bookstore/coffee store. Either way, it would be used for Kingdom purposes.

I drifted back to where Emily Post's *Etiquette* stood on the shelf and pulled it out. I would want to keep this book, no matter what. Suddenly I realized the enormous temptation before me—I now owned thousands of books, and there was a real danger that I would keep far too many of them.

Not many more bookshelves would fit in my apartment, and since I didn't have an office at the college, there would be nowhere to store them except to rent a storage space. And if they were all in storage, what would be the point of keeping them? It was unlikely I would ever need them professionally now, and when I was doing foster care or missionary work I wouldn't be reading them.

An unwelcome sense of loss came over me. It wasn't often I allowed resentment to overtake me, but it was doing so now. I thought of my college friends: most of the girls had married long ago or were successfully following their chosen professions. *Why, Lord? I worked hard and I followed you and now all of my training—all those years of study and hard work—are no longer useful. For what I'll be doing now, I could have just gotten a Bachelor's Degree in General Studies.*

I pushed Emily back into her place more forcefully than I needed to, stalked back to the desk and packed up my stuff. I knew I was giving way to a bad attitude, but I was unwilling to deal with it right now. I wanted a pity party, and I was going to go home and have one.

On Saturday evening I went to pick up Deirdre from her friend's party. She had told me it ended at seven-thirty, but I knew what it was like to be the first to leave a party where your friends are having fun. I thought I'd be just ten minutes late. Not enough to annoy the hosting mom, but also not whisking Deirdre away from the fun too early.

The house was a few miles outside of Wilkester in a lovely country setting. I rang the doorbell of a beautiful modern house—the sort of house that makes you feel underdressed unless you're wearing heels and dangle earrings; I was in jeans and a faded UCSC sweatshirt.

The man who opened the door was nicely dressed, but at least he wasn't in a suit. I felt a bit better.

"Hi, I'm here to pick up Deirdre."

"Oh, hi, I'm Jason. You must be Katrina. Come in. I'll get Deirdre."

"It's very quiet," I said as we walked through the front hall and entered the immense open-plan kitchen-living room. "I expected to see a lot of teenagers with cucumber slices on their eyes."

"You missed that part. The other girls left a little while ago."

"Oh! Am I late? Deirdre said the party would be done

at seven-thirty."

"It was actually seven."

"Oh, dear, I am sorry! I wish Deirdre had called me and let me know. I could have come earlier."

"It was no problem. Tori and Deirdre have been having fun."

"Well, I'm glad she hasn't been in the way. I'm sure you'd like to have the house back to yourselves!"

"No, really, it's ok. I'll go tell Deirdre you're here." He left the room and I could hear him climbing stairs. I looked out the sliding glass doors of the living room. The backyard was an amazing garden of flowers and shrubs. There was even a gazebo. I thought that Becky would like to see it—it was exactly the look she was going for in her backyard.

He came back in. "Deirdre will be a few minutes. I guess they decided to put on some new kind of facial mask and now they have to wash it off."

"Oh! That's fine." I felt like apologizing again but resisted the impulse. I motioned to the garden outside. "Do you guys like to garden? Your backyard is really amazing."

"Thanks. My wife planned the garden but I like to keep it up." He motioned to a barstool at the kitchen island. "Have a seat. I don't think the girls will be too long."

I sat down and tried to think of something to say.

"You have a lovely home," was the first thing that came to mind. "Have you lived here long?"

"We've lived in this house for about ten years. We were in Tacoma before that."

"It's a beautiful area. You must like being out of the city."

"Yes. A little inconvenient for running errands but being in the country is worth it."

We both sat there a little longer. I wondered where

his wife was, but it seemed nosy to ask.

"So, Deirdre is your niece?" said Jason.

"Adopted niece. I've been close friends with her parents for years, so all their kids call me Aunt Katrina."

"That's nice. Deirdre is a really sweet girl. And an amazing artist."

"Oh, you've seen her artwork?"

"Yes, she's in my Saturday art class. One of my best students, actually."

The art teacher! So this was the widowed art teacher she had wanted to set me up with! And she had succeeded in getting me to meet him. *That conniving little…*

"Hi, Aunt Katrina!" Deirdre bounced into the room. She gave me a quick hug but avoided my eyes. "Hey, can we stay and help clean up?"

"Oh, that's not necessary," said Jason. "There's not that much."

"Oh, please?" Tori added her voice. "It's always more fun to clean if there are more people."

"Tori," said Jason, "You shouldn't ask people to help you clean up. Don't feel obliged," he added, turning to me.

"Well, I was the one who offered to help," said Deirdre. "Can we, Aunt Katrina?"

I was stuck. To refuse to help would look ungracious. And if Jason had any inkling of Deirdre's intentions, to insist on helping would look scheming. I erred on the side of graciousness.

"Of course we'll help. It's the least we can do after staying so long."

The girls cheered and I tried to look normal. I knew I was probably not succeeding.

"Well, thanks," said Jason. He didn't seem all that enthusiastic, and I couldn't blame him.

"You hand out the jobs," I said. "We'll do whatever

you say." I was hoping he wouldn't put the two girls working together on something—they would probably make their chore take forever. He likely had the same thought because he asked Deirdre to throw away all the trash—used paper plates, napkins, cucumber slices, lemon rinds and whatever other items had gone into their homemade beauty products—and me to sweep the floor. He took on washing the dishes and made Tori dry them. There was very little talking. By the time Deirdre and I finished our jobs, the others were done, too.

"We need to get going," I said in a tone that I hoped Deirdre knew meant business.

She bade an affectionate farewell to her friend, thanked Jason sweetly for hosting the party, and walked cheerily out to the car with me. Tori stood there waving as we drove away.

I drove only until we were out of sight and then pulled the car over, switched off the engine, and turned to face Deirdre.

"Young lady, that was a manipulative thing to do."

"What?" She said it without much conviction.

"You know exactly what you did. You purposely gave me the wrong time to pick you up, you made sure that you were not ready to go when I got there, and you insisted on us staying to help clean up."

"But—" Deirdre fiddled with her hair. "Are you very mad?"

"I'm trying not to be."

"I was just trying to help."

"I feel manipulated," I said.

"It's just that Tori and I thought you and her dad would be perfect for each other."

"You and Tori."

"Yeah. I was going to get you to come a little late and

we would not be ready. That would give you two a chance to talk. And then I'd offer to help clean up and she would second it, and her dad could see how nice you are. And then afterwards she could ask him what he thought of you."

"Deirdre!" I was horrified. The poor man was a successful artist and widower. Single women my age must have been throwing themselves at him for the past few years. And now he would think I was one of them, probably having engineered the whole encounter. I knew what he would say when Tori asked him what he thought of me: he wasn't interested. "She is tolerable, I suppose, but not handsome enough to tempt me," might even be his exact words. And while there is a sort of tacit rejection whenever a single man doesn't like you, once you have been formally presented to him as a possible wife and are declined, the rejection is more obvious. And painful.

Beyond that, I had explicitly told Deirdre that I wouldn't be interested in dating a widower. Why would she do this to me? To my exasperation, I could feel tears welling up. I was turning into one of those lachrymose females that populated Fanny Burney's novels. At least I hadn't started fainting all the time.

"Oh, Aunt Katrina, *don't cry!*" Deirdre sounded aghast. "I'm so sorry! I didn't know it would bother you that much! Please forgive me!" Her own eyes were spilling over.

I sighed. I couldn't stay upset at someone who was genuinely distressed—someone I'd known since babyhood and had never really wronged me before. I pulled her into a side hug as best I could in my small car. She held me tight.

"It's ok. I forgive you."

She sniffled and I reached into my glove box and pulled out an unused fast food napkin from the stash I keep in there.

"Here you go," I said. "Blow your nose."

She obeyed and wiped her eyes, too. "Are you going to tell my mom?"

"I think *you* should tell her," I said. "If there's any fallout from this I want her to know the situation."

Deirdre nodded sadly. We drove back in silence.

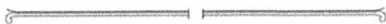

The following week seemed to drag on and on as I graded papers, taught classes and edited an article for a history magazine. I still hadn't shaken the resentment that had descended on my heart, and as for the meeting with the art teacher, I just tried to keep my mind off the subject. I knew things weren't right between me and God, and that my attitude was abysmal, but I wasn't ready to stop sulking yet.

By the time Saturday came around again and Becky and I were sitting in the pew of the Methodist church for the foster care meeting, I had nearly decided to go to Papua New Guinea instead. I just wanted to leave my whole life behind and start over somewhere. All the rest of the people there were couples, which seemed to confirm that foster care wasn't for me.

The first line of George Herbert's "The Collar" recited itself in my head as I sat there: *I struck the board, and cried, "No more; I will abroad!"* It was Herbert's defiance against becoming a clergyman, which, of course, didn't apply to me, and I conveniently forgot the end of the poem.

The lady who got up to speak was a large, cheerful-looking person. She started off explaining the need for families. She painted the picture of abandoned children needing love so clearly that anyone with half a heart would have signed up to be a foster parent on the spot. Then she went on to tell us of the difficulty of the task. The trauma that so many kids came with. The chance for heartbreak, the loneliness, and the stress. That part was painted so clearly that anyone with half a brain would have run the other way. Then she said she was going to interview a woman that had been doing foster care for the last eight years.

It was supposed to be inspirational, I think. The woman shared her journey through infertility and her initial reluctance to take on any children that were not biologically hers. Eventually she was able to let go of the dream she had had for a traditional family and opened her heart to the children in need. It hadn't been all rosy, by any stretch. Her heart had been broken more than once, as well as many items in her house. It was worth it, she said.

She and her husband were very noble, of course, but I was still bothered that her dream of giving birth had never come true. It seemed to me that with so many women in the world unwilling to be mothers at all these days, God ought to have let her give birth to at least one child.

"Wow, that was inspiring, wasn't it?" said Becky when the meeting was over.

"Mm-hmm," I said. I had the feeling that if I thought about it too much I would find out there was some kind of lesson I was supposed to be learning from it, and I wasn't ready to back down yet. Becky signed up for foster care training right away, but I said I needed to pray about it more. I felt a pang of guilt when I said it, realizing that I really hadn't been praying much at all in the last couple of weeks. I pushed the thought aside to deal with later.

On Thursday afternoon I was sitting in the bookstore

preparing for class when Kim texted me.

"Are you at the bookstore? How about I bring you dinner there so we can chat?"

"YES!!!!" I wrote back.

She showed up at five-thirty with fried rice and Mongolian beef from Yang's Yummy House (a name which I suspect sounds better in Chinese). We sat on the floor because the only chair in the place was Frank's desk chair.

"This tastes so good," I said, using my chopsticks to pluck out another piece of beef from the carton.

"Yang's knows how to do it right," agreed Kim.

I was conscious of a disinclination to share what was really going on in my heart. Kim wasn't the kind of friend who would let me alone until I came out of my bad attitude all by myself; she would badger me and cajole me and hit me with Scripture until I could do nothing but repent. I kept our talk confined to how her own kids were doing and her struggle to deal with her cousin's drug problem from two states away.

I thought we were sailing along pretty well with our conversation, and then she said,

"I wanted to invite you over for dinner next Wednesday."

"Sure!"

"There's a catch."

"Ok, what do you need me to do?"

"To sit through dinner and be nice to another guest."

"Who's coming?"

"Jason Evans. Deirdre's art teacher."

I looked at her in disbelief. "Kim, no! I'm sure he already thinks I'm after him after the stunt Deirdre pulled. You can't do that to the poor guy! Invite him to dinner and, 'surprise!' I'm there."

"Hey, hey, hang on. Give me a little credit! I wouldn't do that." Kim looked a little hurt.

"Then what is this?"

"*He* asked *me* to host a dinner where he could get to know you a bit more."

"*Whaaaa?*"

Kim looked entirely too smug. "It was totally his idea."

"But Kim…I already told you. I don't want to date a widower."

"I'm giving you a chance to change your mind."

I shook my head. "Look, if Todd couldn't make me change my mind…" *Oooops.*

Kim's face lit up. "Todd? How does he come into it? Did he say something?"

"He didn't say anything. And I found out he's divorced."

"Why? I mean, why is he divorced?"

"I have no idea."

"But you've ruled him out as a possibility."

"Yes. To put it in your own words, I'm waiting for a Captain Wentworth. Someone who will say 'I have loved none but you.'"

"You also said that if God wanted you to marry a widower, you would."

"Well, He didn't send me a memo telling me I had to marry this one."

"Katrina…"

"Look," I said, losing patience. "I'm not giving God orders, am I? I'm not demanding that he give me the man of my dreams, and that if he doesn't I'm going to grow bitter." I thought it best not to mention that I was currently struggling with resentment. "If He doesn't send me the kind of man I'm willing to marry, I'll happily remain single.

That's not being dictatorial, is it?"

"Oh! So you've decided on the two paths you are willing for your life to take, and God can choose either Plan A or Plan B. He's not free to make an entirely different plan for you?"

"That's not what I'm saying."

"Isn't it?"

I was quiet for a moment. Kim had a point, but I was unwilling to admit it.

"So I have to marry anyone who asks me?" I said belligerently.

Kim shook her head. "You know that isn't what I'm saying. If the man doesn't have the right character, or you don't feel attracted to him, or there is some other impediment like that, then you *shouldn't* marry him. Of course. But what if a woman told you she was only willing to marry a rich man? Or a perfectly fit and healthy man? Or someone with a graduate degree? Would you still be arguing that she was right to hold out for those things in a husband and not consider anyone else?"

I looked at her for a long moment. "You're making too much sense."

"Yes, I know. I'm good at that."

I made a face at her. "It's not like I have a choice to make here anyway. Todd never did ask me out and now I'll probably never see him again. The case is cold. And Jason certainly hasn't asked me to marry him, let alone date him. Besides, a man with a daughter..."

"What's wrong with a man that has a daughter?"

"Are you kidding? Have you not read *Wives and Daughters*?"

"No, but you made me watch the movie. Come on, you could never be a stepmother like Hyacinth. Not even if you tried."

"It's just complicated when there are children."

"Not as complicated as when there are ex-wives with shared custody on top of it."

I goggled at her. "Heavens, I never even thought of that."

"Ok, just say you'll come to dinner. Ed is friends with Jason and the girls are already friends. It's not like a first date with just the two of you."

"And what if he doesn't like me?"

"Then you won't have to make a decision about marrying him."

"That's not what I meant. I just don't want to feel rejected."

Kim pointed her chopsticks at me. "Aha! The truth comes out. This is less a matter of principle for you and more a matter of not getting hurt."

"So? I'm human. I don't want to be hurt."

"Neither does he. But he's taking a risk and testing a possibility. The least you could do is meet him halfway."

I heaved a dramatic sigh. "Fine," I said, "but I'm doing it under protest and just to get you off my back."

"You won't be sorry," she said.

"We'll see," I muttered.

The week seemed to speed up after that; it went by much too quickly for my liking. I dreaded the thought of the dinner at the Coles' (finally, I had something in common with Jane Austen's Emma!) but I was also anxious to get it over with. I wasn't sure which I was more afraid of: Jason deciding he didn't like me enough to pursue me or deciding that he did.

Monday was the April meeting of the library book

club. This time we had read *David Copperfield* and my plan was to talk about the book as a coming of age novel. For some reason, however, the discussion kept coming around to the choices David made in his adult life, particularly his marriage to Dora. Several members of the group admitted that their first infatuation had made them just as blind as David.

"It's odd," said Josephine, who was only seventeen but frequently made the most insightful comments, "but I always thought old books didn't really explore the subject of being with your second love. But this is the third novel this year that has done that."

"That's true," said Gary, a middle-aged trucker who broke every stereotype I had ever believed about truckers. "First there was Laurie in *Little Women*, then there was Marianne in *Sense and Sensibility*, and now this one."

"There are two second-love stories in *Sense and Sensibility*," said the lady whose name I can never remember. "Marianne was also Col. Brandon's second love."

"They aren't quite the same, though, are they?" I put in. "There's quite a disparity in the characters if you think about it. Marianne didn't marry Willoughby, but he was not worthy of her love—quite a bad guy, in fact. When Laurie didn't marry Jo, she wasn't a bad girl, just not the right girl for him. And David Copperfield did actually marry Dora, who wasn't bad either, but not the best match for him. And if Col. Brandon had married Eliza, they might have had a very happy marriage, but of course we'll never know."

"That's not quite what I was getting at," said Josephine. "I was just saying none of them were married to their first love by the end of the novel, and yet each one had what you might call a perfect match. I thought that was more of a modern concept, but I guess I was wrong."

"Yeah," said a guy named Brady who rarely spoke. "I

thought classic novels always promoted the one-and-only love idea. I'm glad they don't."

In desperation I turned the conversation toward a comparison of Uriah Heep and Mr. Micawber and kept it there until it was time to go. But afterwards I sat in my car in the parking lot and stared into the darkness. Francis Thompson had not been kidding when he called God "the hound of heaven." I now knew what it felt like to be hunted. I grabbed my phone and looked up the poem; I hadn't memorized all one hundred and eighty-two lines and I wanted to read it again.

> I fled Him, down the nights and down the days;
> I fled Him, down the arches of the years;
> I fled Him, down the labyrinthine ways
> Of my own mind; and in the mist of tears
> I hid from Him, and under running laughter.
> Up vista'd hopes I sped;
> And shot, precipitated,
> Adown Titanic glooms of chasm'd fears,
> From those strong Feet that followed, followed after.
> But with unhurrying chase,
> And unperturbèd pace,
> Deliberate speed, majestic instancy,
> They beat—and a Voice beat
> More instant than the Feet—
> 'All things betray thee, who betrayest Me.'
> I pleaded, outlaw-wise,
> By many a hearted casement, curtained red,
> Trellised with intertwining charities;
> (For, though I knew His love Who followèd,
> Yet was I sore adread
> Lest, having Him, I must have naught beside).

I stopped there. That was what I was afraid of: that if I surrendered my plans I would have nothing. I would be stuck in a pathetic life—perhaps one even more pathetic than my current one. And all I would have would be God.

And what would be wrong with that?

"All right, Lord, I can take a hint," I said aloud, then shook my head. A hint? This was not a hint. It was a bash over the head. I tried again. "You win, God. I know that trying to thwart Your plan is useless. Whatever You decide to do happens, no matter how much I wish for it to be different." I stopped again. I was making God sound like blind, malignant Fate. "I know you do everything for my good," I went on, "and it will all work out in the end. But the thought still terrifies me. Please, please, can you make it be not too bad? I'm scared."

It could not have been called a glad surrender or even a wholehearted repentance. It was, however, the first crack in my defences.

The dinner went off better than I would have expected. Kim and Ed had ordered pizza, and we all sat around their living room and stuffed ourselves. Deirdre must have been given explicit instructions about what she could and could not say, because no embarrassing comments or questions came from her. She and Tori stuck together like glue.

Jason asked me a few get-to-know-you questions and seemed genuinely interested in what I had to say, but he spent more time talking to Ed than to me, which was quite a relief. I couldn't tell if I could be attracted to him or not. He was nice-enough looking, and a friendly guy, but I wasn't sure I could like him as more than a friend. I told myself firmly that it didn't matter right now, and turned my attention to Josh, who was suggesting we all play Clue.

"There's too many people," Deidre objected. "It's only for six people and we have twelve."

"We could do teams," said Tori.

Sam and Ben put in their vote for playing with teams, and the adults capitulated. It seemed I couldn't get away from murder, even in my leisure time.

"I'll get it set up," said Josh, and departed to the games cabinet.

"By the way," Kim told me as we cleared the table for the game, "would you be willing to help with the foster families' Fun Day this year? It's the first Saturday in May."

"Sure, that's right after the semester ends. What are they doing this time?"

"It's a treasure hunt in the woods, near your favorite spot."

"Oh that'll be fun. I just hope it doesn't rain."

"Well, that's always a risk, isn't it? It's what we get for living in Washington. We'll have some things we can do even if the weather's bad."

Josh came over to the table with the game just then and he and Mia set it up. We all drew names for teams and then crowded as best we could around the table. I was paired with Sam, who was far more competitive about it than I was.

"Who do you think did it, Aunt Katrina?" he whispered after we'd all taken several turns.

"I still don't know," I whispered back.

"I wish we had a real detective here," he grumbled.

So do I, I thought, and then wanted to kick myself. Even if I was willing to consider being someone's second love, Todd was still not Our Kind of Person. That was a character issue, and it wasn't something I could ignore. I forced myself to focus on the game.

CHAPTER 10

On Thursday morning there was an email from Sheila in my inbox.

"I'm rewriting the last three chapters," the email said, "and I have a question. Would it be the butler or the housekeeper who would be in charge of decanting wines?"

That was a good question. I was pretty sure I knew the answer if the setting were in England, but I wasn't sure about the colonies. Of course the jobs of servants in the two places were almost identical, but there was always the chance this might be one of the things that was different. In fact, hadn't there been a reference to decanting wine in that American butler's memoirs I had thumbed through while Cassie was reading *Modern Chivalry*? The thing was, he did mention the housekeeper more than once and I couldn't be sure it wasn't in connection with the wine. I decided it would be best if I checked it out.

Accordingly, after class I went to the library. Emily the librarian unlocked the Special Collections room and the book cabinet and left me to my research. It took me about fifteen minutes to find the passage I had seen:

"When I arose from my sickbed I found that the housekeeper had taken it upon herself to decant the wine. From ignorance she did not use a wine-strainer with fine cambric in it, and some bits of crust and cork got into it. I was reproved for (as it seemed) my carelessness, but did not betray the housekeeper, for which she earnestly thanked me later."

That was good enough for me to give an answer about it to Sheila. I put the book back and headed toward the door to tell Emily she could lock up again. I paused at the Bradstreet manuscript on my way out to read it one more time. For some reason it looked different to me, and I thought it must be the lighting. I glanced up at the ceiling, but the lights were all on, and seemed as bright as usual. I looked at the poem again. In a moment I saw what was different. The water stains were gone.

Did they get it cleaned? I wondered. I looked closely at it. I thought the margins might be a little wider than they had been before.

I went out of the room and found the librarian.

"Emily, did the library do something with the Bradstreet manuscript?" I said.

"What do you mean? It's still there. I saw it when I unlocked for you," she said.

"I know, but it's changed," I said. "The water stains that were along one side are gone. And I think the margins on the sides of the writing are larger than they were."

She came with me into the Special Collections room and looked at the manuscript.

"I think you're right. This isn't the same manuscript. It's a forgery." She could hardly have sounded more horror-struck. "How did it get in here? And where's the real manuscript?"

"It must have been stolen," I said. "And someone replaced it with this so it wouldn't be noticed."

"Oh no," she breathed. I knew how she felt. She was one of the people responsible for the document.

"You need to call the police," I said. "It's a valuable

item."

The police. I felt a little sick to my stomach. I thought I was finished with making statements to the police. And Todd. Well, hopefully they would send someone else. The police department had more than one detective.

I stood by while Emily made the call.

"They want whoever discovered it to stay here until they get here," she said after she hung up. "I hope that's ok."

"Yes, I can stick around. I guess I should sit here and grade some rough drafts while I'm waiting." I opened my laptop and started reading through the papers. I read through them with only half my brain engaged. The other half of my brain kept praying, "Dear Lord, please let them send Detective Ortega."

"Are you Emily Watkins? I'm Detective Mason with the Wilkester Police Department."

I closed my eyes and groaned inwardly. *Once more into the breach*, I thought. With a sigh I closed my laptop and put it into my bag.

"I need to speak to whoever discovered the theft," said Todd. Emily nodded toward me as I was coming over to the front desk.

I cleared my throat. "That would be me, Detective Mason."

There was a flicker of surprise on his face, but all he said was, "Ah, Miss Peters. How nice to see you again. Do you think you could show me where the incident occurred?"

The three of us trooped back to the Special Collections room. I pointed to the glass case.

"That is where the manuscript was. There's a manuscript there right now, but it's not the same one."

"How did you know this one was different?"

"A few things," I said. "The biggest is the water stains—I mean the lack of water stains. The original had a pattern of water stains down the right side of it, kind of light, but you could definitely see them. Also, I think the margins are different—wider than they were on the other document."

"And the writing?"

"It looks pretty much the same, actually. Whoever made this copy was very, very good at writing like people did in the sixteen hundreds."

"Is anything else missing?"

"Oh, I have no idea," said Emily. "I never thought to check. I can get the list of books that should be here…" she paused.

"What's the matter?" I asked.

"Well, if any of them are replaced with forgeries, I don't think I will be able to tell. I don't know the books inside and out, physically—I haven't spent that much time studying them. In fact, I'm not sure I would have even noticed the difference in the Bradstreet manuscript if Professor Peters hadn't pointed it out. I mean, after she said something I remembered that there were some water stains on the manuscript, but I probably wouldn't have thought about it on my own."

"So," said Todd, making a note of what she had said, "You don't know when the real manuscript was replaced with the forgery?"

Emily shook her head.

"I know the real one was here a few weeks ago. Remember when I came with a student to the Special Collections room to see *Modern Chivalry*?" I asked Emily.

"Yes, that's right," said Emily.

"Do you remember exactly when that was?" asked Todd.

I tried to think. "It was a few days after the—the murder."

Todd wrote that down. "How hard would it be for someone to get in that room to replace the manuscript?"

"Well, we keep it locked, and of course the building has an alarm at night."

"And the glass case has a lock as well, I see. Are all the keys on the same key ring?"

Emily nodded. "Is that bad?"

"Not necessarily. Where do you keep the keys?"

"In the desk drawer—the front desk, where we check out books."

"Could anyone get at them?"

Emily looked like she was wilting. "Well, I guess they could. But it would be kind of hard. I mean, that's the desk that the two senior librarians and the assistants use. But only the senior librarians are allowed to use those keys and let people into the room. And there has to be either a professor or a librarian present with anyone going into the room. And the desk where the keys are—it's very visible. When the library is open there's always someone working there, except for maybe just a second, going to check something. It would be hard for someone to sneak into the desk and get them without being noticed."

"I see. Well, I'm going to need to see your records of who has been in this room in the last five weeks."

"Oh dear," said a dismayed Emily. "I'm afraid we don't write down who goes in. I can tell you everyone I remember, but you'll have to ask the other library staff, too."

"All right." He seemed so much more somber than usual, and I felt like we had disappointed him. He finished writing and closed his notebook. "We'll have to lock up the room and I'll send a team to do the usual sweep." He turned to Emily. "It would be good if you got the list of books now and made sure nothing else is missing."

"Sure. But what if one of them is a forgery? I probably won't know."

"Would you be able to tell, Miss Peters?" he said.

"If it was a badly done forgery, I would. If it was a very, very clever one you'd need to get a lab to verify things. But I find it hard to believe someone would try to forge one of those books. They aren't particularly valuable, and the time and effort it would take to forge a whole book would be considerable. One sheet of paper like the Bradstreet poem is possible, but a whole book would be only worth doing if it was extremely precious—and these aren't."

"I suspect you're right," said Todd. "Would you be free now to just glance through them?"

"What about fingerprints?"

"You've already been in here, probably several times during the year, correct? So your fingerprints are probably on the cabinet and books anyway. Like you said, I doubt those books were tampered with. Just don't touch the glass case." He paused. "Did you touch the case today?"

"I don't remember," I said. "I might have. I don't know." I felt guilty. In our previous meetings, Todd had seemed to go out of his way to be reassuring. Today he just seemed detached and maybe a little cold. No one could have called him rude, but I could tell there was a difference.

He hung around while Emily and I checked the books against her list and I duly flipped through each one. They were all there and all looked genuine.

"Is that all?" said Emily

"It is for now. I need to get the word out on this one—notify dealers in manuscripts and old books, in case the thief tries to sell it. I hope it's not too late. We don't know when it was stolen, but it might have been weeks ago."

"Surely anyone in the book trade would recognize it for what it is—and even if they didn't they could certainly trace who bought it."

"If they sold it through official channels, yes. But if the thief sold it to a private collector…" Todd's voice trailed off.

"I see," I said. "But if they did that, what difference would it make if it was newly stolen or not?"

"Well, we have informants that could find out if there is any chatter about it in the underground collectors' world."

"It sounds very CIA," I said. I thought Todd smiled faintly, but he said nothing.

"I'd better get back to work," said Emily. "I'll get the other librarian to write down everyone they can remember going into the room in the last few weeks, and I'll do it, too."

"Yes, thank you," said Todd. "I'll be in touch tomorrow, and my team should be here in the morning to see if they can discover anything from the room and case itself." He gave Emily his card. "Please let me know if you remember anything that might be helpful. Otherwise I'll talk to you tomorrow." He turned to me. "I may have a few questions for you as the investigation progresses, but for now you're free to go. Thanks for your help." He shook my hand, and I thought he held it a fraction of a moment longer than he needed to. It might have been my imagination.

Kim called as soon as I got home.

"Hi Katrina, how are you?"

I made a quick decision not to tell her about the manuscript theft right away. I didn't want her to start worrying about this sudden crime wave in Wilkester.

"I'm fine. How are you guys?"

"Busy. I meant to call you yesterday but it was such a crazy day and this is the first moment I've had to talk."

"What's up?"

"I need information from you."

"About what?"

"The dinner two nights ago." She heard me snort and went on rapidly. "I'm not trying to be pushy! In fact, I made up my mind not to bring it up unless you did. But I can't bear it any longer. I promise not to badger you about it, but I just have to know what you think of Jason."

"I'm shocked you were able to make it this long without interrogating me. No, really! I am pleasantly surprised. You have amazing self-control."

"I'm working on it. But I have none left now. Spill it."

"Well…" I sighed. "I don't know what to think. He's a nice guy. Not repulsive or anything. But I didn't feel any sparks between us—although I suppose it would be nearly impossible for that to happen at such an awkward gathering."

"Awkward? Really?"

"Not you guys. But I was self-conscious and he might have been too, and you can't make a valid judgement of someone when you're distracted like that."

"Fair enough," said Kim. "But he's not a definite no, right?"

"I suppose not."

"Good. I won't say another word about it unless he makes a move."

"Thanks. Oh, and Kim, you want me to take Ben and Mia out for a McDonald's run?"

"That would be great! They've been struggling this week and we're all a little weary. I won't tell them beforehand in case they get too excited, but just let me know what is a good time for you."

"How about tonight? I'll pick them up at five o'clock and take them to dinner."

"Fantastic! Thanks so much."

We said our goodbyes and hung up. I'd started taking the Coles' foster kids for a McDonald's run occasionally back when they first started fostering. It gave the parents (and their biological offspring) a break from walking on eggshells around the traumatized children and a chance to do things together without the foster kids being jealous. And it made the kids feel special and loved by someone outside of their foster family. I'd had to be approved as someone who could babysit foster kids, but it was worth it.

I showed up at five o'clock and announced that I was going to McDonald's for dinner and needed two kids to come with me. Mia and Ben practically ran me over in their eagerness to get to my car. It took a few minutes to transfer car seats and boosters to my vehicle, and I thought that it might not be too long before I needed to buy car seats for my own foster kids. If I didn't go to Papua New Guinea. Or marry Jason.

Watch it, I told myself. *Don't start thinking like that.*

I buckled the kids into their seats and zipped down the road toward Tacoma. Of course Wilkester has its own McDonald's—in fact, there are two— but driving to Tacoma makes the experience last longer. I put in my CD of kids Scripture songs, and we sang our way into the big city. When Mia had arrived at the Coles' her vocabulary seemed to consist mostly of expletives, the legacy from her former environment. And here she was, singing at the top of her lungs:

> "The Lord has done
> Great things for us,
> We are glad
> We are glad, glad, glad
> Oh, oh, oh
> The Lord has done
> Great things for us,
> We are glad."

Her childish little voice earnestly singing the Oh, oh, oh, in the middle was so stinkin' cute I could hardly stand it. It was sweet to think about the contrast between the life of abuse and neglect both kids had come from and the life they had now. It was not perfect, but they were in a place of life and hope. The Lord had indeed done great things for them. I was so grateful to be part of it even in a very small way.

Both kids wanted to eat inside the restaurant instead of going through the drive-through. Unfortunately, when we got inside we found that the line was pretty long. I suggested we go back to the car and order in the drive-through, but they both insisted that they would rather stand in line.

Before we were halfway through our line, Mia started trying to run around the restaurant. I picked her up and held her, singing silly songs and bouncing her along with them to distract her. It worked, but by the time we got to the front of the line, I thought my arms would fall off. She was a petite little thing, but thirty-five pounds of squirming five-year-old is more than I am used to carrying. The length of the wait had given both kids enough time to change their minds about their order three times apiece, but in the end they both wanted a kids' meal with chicken nuggets.

"I want a Coke to drink!" said Ben.

"No, your mom says only juice, remember?" I used my best loving-Auntie voice.

"Coke!" echoed Mia.

I went ahead and ordered the juice. As I paid for the meals, I saw Mia's lip tremble.

"Hey," I said brightly, "Why don't the two of you pick out where you want to sit!"

"I choose!" shouted Ben and ran off with Mia yelling "Noooooo!" right behind him.

I grabbed our tray of food and pursued them as quickly as I could. Ben landed at a table next to the giant plate-glass window. There was an empty table next to his, and Mia seated herself there, looking very pleased with herself. I prayed the restaurant wouldn't fill up any more; I could imagine the dirty looks we would get if someone needed a seat and there was Mia taking up a whole table by herself. I knew that trying to move her right now would set off a tantrum. The excitement of being out with Aunt Katrina was proving to be too much for them to handle.

Ben snatched at his meal box and opened it to get the toy out. It was a little plastic figure of Zed, the cartoon character from a recent movie. Mia plunged into her box and pulled out a little spaceship from the same movie.

"Ok, now, let's eat," I said. "I'll say grace." I bowed my head and said a short prayer of thanks, knowing that anything longer than a sentence would be too much for their diminished self-control.

Ben ate a couple of nuggets and then noticed his drink.

"I wanted Coke," he pouted.

"Juice is good," I said as cheerfully as I could. He

steadily ate French fries for a few minutes but kept looking over at Mia's toy. Mia had stopped eating completely and was zooming her little spaceship around.

"Let's eat, Mia," I said. "See if you can make those nuggets disappear!"

She condescended to eat one and went back to playing.

"How come she got that one and I didn't?" was Ben's next comment.

"I don't know. They just put different ones in your boxes."

Ben crossed his arms and kicked the table leg. "I don't want Zed. I want the spaceship!"

"It's a great toy!" I enthused. "Lots of kids would like it."

"It's not fair!" he said more loudly. "Why did I get Zed?"

"Listen," I said, lowering my voice in hopes that it would prompt him to lower his, too, "God is in charge of everything—every single little thing—and *He* picked that toy out for you!" Practical theology for kids, that's what it was. Ben was not impressed.

"I don't want it!" he yelled. He picked up Zed, marched over to the trash can, and threw the toy in.

"Ok, we need to get going," I said. I've seen the wind-up to Ben's tantrums more than once and that's exactly where this was headed. The only thing I could do was make sure the good patrons of McDonald's were not subjected to a front-row view of it. I got as much food as I could back into the boxes (my own burger had been hardly touched) and tried to comfort Mia who was now wailing, "But I *want* to eat here!"

Somehow I struggled out the door juggling the boxes of food and hanging onto Mia and praying that Ben wouldn't chose this moment to run. He was screaming now, saying words that no seven-year-old should know, but at least he was walking with us. *See that single mom with those brats?* I could imagine the onlookers thinking. *That's what happens when you have no discipline in the home.*

I got the kids strapped into their car seats and got into my seat and breathed a sigh of relief. The child locks on the doors meant that Ben couldn't get out and run away, no matter how upset he got. He was screaming and crying and flailing around and Mia was just crying because she'd had to leave Mc.Donald's without eating much of her food. I was afraid to give her any—Ben might knock it out of her hand or something. I'd have to wait until he calmed down.

The drive back to Wilkester was the reverse of the trip to Tacoma in more ways than one. Instead of the car being filled with happy praise songs to God there was rage and cursing. I knew it was a result of the trauma Ben had experienced in his short life, but it was still incredible to me. When he'd arrived at Ed and Kim's home he was malnourished and physically abused. He had no belongings—not a single item that he could call his own. Even the clothes he was wearing were donated from the fostering agency. The Coles had given him love. They had given him clothing, toys, and books. They had played games with him, fed him well, and told him about Jesus. And now, when he was being given a special treat by someone who had no obligation to do anything for him, he was bitter and angry because he didn't get the same cheap plastic toy as his sister. Couldn't he even remember the song we'd been singing less than an hour ago?

"The Lord has done
Great things for us,
We are glad."

And are you any better? said the voice in my head. Look at what the Lord has done for you. You were transferred from the kingdom of darkness to the kingdom of God. You were a child of Satan and now are a child of God. You were forgiven the mountain of sins that should have sent you to hell. You were blessed with every spiritual blessing in Christ. You have a home in heaven and eternal joy waiting for you. And here you are, getting bitter and saying it's not fair because you're not getting the same circumstances as someone else. Just like Ben, you want to reject the life God picked out especially for you.

It was, in some ways, a terrible moment. There is nothing so humbling as realizing you have been acting like a hysterical seven-year-old—worse, actually, because your understanding is so much greater than his and you don't have the excuse of a trauma-injured brain.

"I'm sorry, Lord," I whispered. "I am so, so sorry." The last of my defences crumbled, and I felt like Mia, running with outstretched arms toward the one she loves. And His arms were outstretched too. Ben was still shrieking and Mia's sobs sounded like hiccups, but the noise might have been Brahms' lullaby for all the effect it had on my newly-peaceful soul.

CHAPTER 11

When I finished teaching American Lit the next day, Todd was waiting for me outside the classroom.

"Well, well," I quipped. "Just like old times."

The charming smile appeared for just a moment. "Hello, Miss Peters. I'm afraid I need to ask you to come down to the station again. I have some questions to ask you about the missing manuscript."

"Sure," I said, wondering what else I could possibly be asked about.

He drove me to the station without any small talk, and it made me uneasy. I was ushered into one of the old familiar interrogation rooms.

"It's odd how I keep getting involved in these crimes," I said as we sat down. "I've gone my whole life without any contact with law enforcement, other than one speeding ticket when I first got my license. Witnessing one crime was extraordinary. Being a kind of witness to a second crime is almost unbelievable. I'm surprised I haven't been arrested as the likeliest suspect."

He remained silent, looking down at his notebook. A cold feeling began to settle in my stomach.

"I am a suspect? *Again*?"

He looked up at me. The expression in his eyes was no longer aloof. I thought he looked pained.

"If you could just answer a few questions for me?"

I managed to nod.

"When did you first learn about the Bradstreet manuscript?"

I took a deep breath. "You mean that it existed? In college. I heard about it when it was discovered. We don't have anything else that is in Bradstreet's own handwriting. She wrote the poems in America in the 1640s, and her brother-in-law had them printed without her knowledge in London in 1650."

"Was she upset?"

"It seems she was more than a little frustrated. She hadn't had the chance to get the poems just the way she wanted them for print—it's the way any author would feel if their rough first draft was published before they could polish it up. About twenty-five years later she had it re-published in Boston with her own corrections and additions. This manuscript that was stolen seems to have been made at that time. Whether it was one of the fair copies sent to the printer or one made for her children we don't know."

"Hang on," said Todd. "What's a fair copy?"

"Oh! It just means a perfect copy with no mistakes. You know, if you have to write things by hand in pen you make mistakes, cross them out, put in a word with an arrow where you forgot one—that kind of thing. And of course if you write with quill ink, you can't erase any mistakes. So a fair copy was one that looked perfect, and a printer could use it to make up the plates of type for the printing press."

"I see. Go on."

"This manuscript—just the one poem—turned up in the effects of one of her great, great, great…I don't know how many greats it is. But one of her descendants, anyway. She had lots; eight children and forty-seven grandchildren and you can imagine how many each generation added to the number."

"It's amazing it lasted through that many generations and didn't get sold or something along the way."

"Well, her poetry was out of fashion for centuries, so there wouldn't have been much market for it. It was preserved in an old family Bible for part of that time, at least."

"And it was discovered how?"

"Whichever descendant it was that had owned it died in about 1997. They had a big enough collection of old books and things that they were all auctioned off. Someone bought a few of the books, including the Bible, and when they got it home they found the manuscript inside. The man had it authenticated and everything."

"And the college bought it from him?"

"No, it was bought by Willard L. Jackson, who then later donated all the books in that Special Collections room. His portrait is the one hanging in there."

"And you told me it's worth a lot of money. Do you know how much?"

"No. Several thousand dollars at least, I'm sure. I don't know how much Mr. Jackson paid for it and that was well over twenty years ago, so the price would probably be different now. I'm sure the librarians could tell you what it's worth."

Todd spent a moment writing, and then looked up.

"Do you know the code to turn off the library alarm?"

"Goodness, no. I don't even think full professors know that. I'd say the only people that would know it would be the librarians and the security staff. Possibly some other administrators. The library is connected to the administration building, you know, and it's probably the same code for all of it. Or maybe not," I said, frowning. "Wouldn't it be better to have separate codes?"

"I can't say," said Todd, and wrote some more in his notebook. Finally he put down his pen and ran his fingers through his hair.

"I'm sorry to have dragged you in for more questioning today. The fact is, I got in a little bit of trouble for not having you searched yesterday, and I was ordered to investigate you a little more thoroughly."

"*Searched!* What for?"

"The manuscript."

I just stared at him.

"Look at it from the chief's point of view: it would have been extremely easy for you to do the crime. You were in the room by yourself. You know enough about forgeries and literature and particularly that manuscript to make up a fake. It wouldn't have to be perfect, just good enough to make it look like it was supposed to be. You go in the room alone, pick the lock on the case or else use a key you'd somehow gotten a duplicate of, switch the manuscripts and conceal the real one under your jacket or something. You raise the alarm, slip the paper into your bag, and walk away with it. You could sell it on the black market and add to your meagre salary."

"But—but—I would never—"

"I know that, Miss Peters. But recall that you were cleared from suspicion in Frank's murder due to lack of evidence against you, not because you had an alibi."

"You mean you think the crimes are connected?"

"They may be. Don't forget that Frank asked you about forgeries. It wasn't the property deed he meant—we know that now—so it might have been something to do with this."

"So now what?"

"Now we wait to see if the real manuscript turns up for sale. And we investigate the people that the librarians remember letting into the room. For example, we need to see if Kevin Schmidt was ever in there. He might be connected to both crimes—maybe he thought he could use the money from the sale of the manuscript to hide some of his bad financial dealings at the college."

"Can I – I mean, if there's anything I can do to help, will you let me know?"

He smiled slightly and I immediately felt like an idiot. What in the world could I do—look for suspicious characters and follow them around?

"That was a stupid thing for me to say," I blurted. "Never mind."

He shook his head. "Not stupid. I don't think I've ever heard you say something stupid."

"Stick around, then," I said. "Spend enough time with me and you'll hear something before long." It took me a second to realize what I'd said. *Did I really just tell him to spend time with me?* I could feel my ears turning red.

He murmured something that I thought sounded like "Don't mind if I do." He rose from his chair and said more loudly, "You're free to go. And we'll let you know if we need your help."

"Ok," I said, and made my escape.

A couple days later I got a letter from Frank's lawyer saying that the will had been proven, and the title deed to the bookstore was now in my name. I met Becky for dinner that day in a heavily distracted frame of mind. She was all excited about starting the classes for foster care and I was beginning to panic about making the decisions I had deferred until the store was actually mine. Now that it was, I was going to have to look at the possibilities in earnest.

"I don't know," I moaned when she asked me if I was going to do foster care. I slumped pathetically in the restaurant booth. "Sometimes I think foster care is something I really want to do. But then my friend Carrie who teaches at the mission school wrote to me a couple days ago asking if I had decided to go there next year. The kids that are her students—it's a mix of missionary kids and national kids—are so sweet. A couple of them have special needs, and they might be able to give them more support if I'm there. If they don't get another teacher for the fall, they'll really be stretched to their limit and may have to turn some national kids away. That makes me think I ought to go. I mean, lots of people could do foster care, but not many could go to the mission field. And then I worry that I'm going to rush into things and make a bad decision."

"Well, let's look at this logically," said Becky. "Just what are your options?"

"The way I see it, I have three. One is that I sell the bookstore and use the money to fund my missionary venture. Another is that I stay here and do foster care. I could sell the books in the bookstore to a dealer and let our church use the building to start a Christian bookstore-coffee shop that aims to attract college students and other people in the town. The third option is that I just do what I'm doing for another year, and either sell the bookstore and books and keep the money for later or sell just the books and do the coffee shop idea. That would keep me from making a snap decision I might later regret. And keeping the status quo for a year seems to be the prudent course. But I don't really want to do the same thing for another whole year! And would I really regret either of those other options?"

"I see what you mean. What do your parents think?"

"They think I should keep doing what I'm already doing, but they don't really feel strongly one way or the other. And the thing is, I can come up with arguments on both sides. I read verses in the Proverbs that talk about not making hasty decisions, and I also read verses that say we should make the most of our time because the days are evil. I wish God would send me a clear message telling me what to do. I have a month to decide about PNG."

"PNG?"

"Papua New Guinea. Oh! And I have another decision to make: I have this book that I have to figure out what to do with." I explained about Matthew Wilke's journal. "I feel like by suppressing the truth, I'm a party to a fraud. If I sell the journal to the family, they will probably hide it or destroy it. If I sell it to someone else or give it to the town museum, I'm sure the true facts will come out, and I will feel like I betrayed the Wilkes family. I really don't have anything against them."

"Hmmm, that's a tough one," said Becky. "But I think you're right; suppressing the truth is being party to a fraud. After all, Matt knows the truth and so do the police. The honest thing for the Wilkes family to do is to come clean about it. They've already been given the chance to do that. Maybe you should write them a letter, explaining that you're going to give the journal to the town museum— which is what I think you should do—and giving them a chance to set the record straight before someone else makes a big story about it."

"I feel like they'll hate me," I said. "I don't want to feel like their enemy."

"You can't let that stop you from doing what's right," said Becky.

"I don't like making a fuss," I pouted. "Live and let

live is my style. I didn't even make a stink when I was let go from UCSC unfairly. And yet here I am, mixed up in fraud and murder and theft…"

"Almost as if God wanted to shake you up a bit." Becky grinned.

"He's succeeded," I said. "By the way, Kim sent me some toys for you. Someone gifted her a big box of play stuff and she said she already has enough. She thought you might be able to use them when you start fostering. I've got them in my car for you."

"Great! I'm getting my spare room all decked out as a kids room. I could use some more toys."

After we'd finished our meal and paid our bill, Becky came with me to my car.

"I need to organize and clean out my trunk," I said as I unlocked and opened it. The large box of toys had barely fit into the space, cluttered as it was with a bag I kept forgetting to take to the thrift store, a car jack, jumper cables, a soccer ball, and a crate of miscellaneous items with the books Todd had given me from Frank's house perched on top.

"Wow, those look old," said Becky, pointing to the books.

"They are," I said. "I should have taken them into the store a few weeks ago. I just keep forgetting." I looked at the books and felt like they were a perfect illustration of my ineptness. I had these major, life-altering decisions to make and all I was doing was mentally going in circles and blubbering "I don't know what to do!" over and over. How could anyone as ineffectual as I make an actual difference in anyone's life? I couldn't even remember to put things away where they belonged.

"Hey," said Becky, sensing my discouragement. "In our weakness He is strong." She pulled me into a hug.

"Trust that God will guide you. He won't let you miss His will if you are eager to find it."

"Right," I said. I could feel some of the stress departing. "Thanks for reminding me."

"No problem. And tell Kim thanks for the toys."

Right on cue, my phone rang.

"Ha!" I said. "It's Kim."

"I'll let you chat," said Becky, giving me a quick goodbye hug and leaving me to answer my call.

"Hey, Kim."

"Katrina! You need to get over here *right now*."

"What's wrong?" I said, visions of Ben or Mia gone missing racing through my mind.

"You didn't tell me about this manuscript theft! Ed just informed me that you were the one who discovered it!"

"Oh, is that all? I didn't want to worry you."

"Worry, shmurry," she said. "You just didn't want me to ask which detective was in charge of the case."

"Well, I—"

"Never mind. You need to get over here anyway because I have to talk to you about the Fun Day you said you'd help with. You can fill me in on the theft at the same time."

"To hear is to obey," I said.

"That's what I like to hear," she said and hung up.

The Cole home was somewhat chaotic when I arrived. Houdini the dog had gotten out again, Sam and Ben were arguing over whose turn it was to load the dishwasher, and Mia was sobbing because Josh was out looking for Houdini instead of playing a promised game of Uno with her.

"Welcome to the madhouse," said Kim. "And Deirdre's friend Kelsey is coming over soon to work on a history project."

"Change of plans," said Deirdre, coming into the room. "Kelsey's grounded. I'm going to have to go to her house. Can Dad take me?"

"You can ask him," said Kim. "What did Kelsey do wrong?"

"She lied to her parents. She said she was out with her cousin Matt but she was really out with her boyfriend—the one she's grounded from seeing outside of school. She's been doing it for weeks, I guess. Every Tuesday at three o'clock. She said she and Matt were going out to practice driving, but she was really driving around with her boyfriend."

Kim sighed. "That girl."

"I know," said Deirdre. "She doesn't learn very well."

Kim settled the dispute between the boys, making them work together to load the dishwasher and giving them an extra chore to work on besides. Josh came home with Houdini and started the card game with Mia, and Ed took Deirdre to her friend's house. Peace descended on the household. Kim made us both a cup of tea and led me over to the dining room table to work on plans for the Fun Day.

"First, tell me about this theft. All I know is that a valuable manuscript was taken and you are the star witness."

"I don't know about 'star witness' but I was the one who noticed that the manuscript lying there in the glass case was different than the one that had been there before."

"And who is the policeman assigned to the case?"

"Detective Mason." I tried to sound nonchalant.

Kim smirked.

"Ok, now what is this about the Fun Day?" I said before she could make any disturbing comments. "You said it was going to be a treasure hunt."

"Well, that's the theme. But it's not quite like a

scavenger hunt. That was the original plan, but when it came down to it, 'find a pinecone' was going to be too easy and 'spot a woodpecker' might be too hard. And we didn't want families picking rare wildflowers or anything. So we've modified it. The families will follow markers to different stations, where they'll have to complete a challenge as a family team and earn a ticket. I think there will be eight different stations. You'll be at one of the stations, explaining what the families need to do and giving them their ticket at the end of it. There'll be two helpers at each station, in case of emergencies. You know, like if someone gets hurt or lost or something."

"Just how dangerous is this stuff supposed to be?"

She laughed. "Not dangerous at all. It's just an abundance of caution. And then when the challenges are all completed, you can help serve the food—there's supposed to be a cookout with hotdogs and hamburgers."

"And what will you do if it rains?"

"We'll keep going with the challenges—which reminds me, have an umbrella and a rain jacket in your car—and we'll move the dinner to a few different houses. We've divided up the families into three groups, and each one can go to a different house where we'll just cook hamburgers on the stove and boil the hotdogs. Not as good as a barbeque, but better than no food at all. Hopefully we won't have to do that—we'll only move to that plan if it's really pouring rain and we can't light a fire at all. We have some canopies we can put up for people to eat under if it's only a light drizzle."

"Sounds good."

"Now, my job is coming up with prizes we can give out. They can't be too expensive, obviously, and they can't all be the same. We thought we'd give prizes for all kinds of things, so that every family had a real chance at winning something. We need to keep it under about four dollars apiece."

"Baked goods? Or homemade mixes for baked goods? That would be a lot faster and easier than baking them up ourselves."

"I like it! What else?"

"Homemade bubble solution and wands?"

In half an hour we came up with a dozen nice-but-cheap items we could use as prizes.

"I'd better get home," I said. "I have class to teach in the morning, and I have to write a letter to Matt's family, telling them that I'm going to offer the journal to the Wilkester Museum. They'll probably hate me for it, but I refuse to try to make money off the book by selling it, and I also refuse to be party to a continuing lie by suppressing it. So I don't have much choice."

"I'll pray they take it well," said Kim she walked me to the front door. "One more thing…Jason wanted your phone number. I gave it to him."

"Oh!" I stopped walking.

"Are you ok with that?"

I sighed. "I guess so. I mean, you could hardly refuse to give it to him after I said he wasn't a definite no."

"Exactly." She patted me on the shoulder. "Don't look so tragic. It's a good thing, right?"

"I just don't want to start anything if it isn't going to work out."

"Sorry. There aren't any money-back guarantees. Just take the next step."

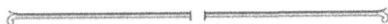

After class the next day, I went to the bookstore to do the writing of the letter as well as grade the final papers for the English 90 class. I was going to miss this place, I thought as I let myself in and flicked on the lights. Whatever happened, I wouldn't be keeping it as my private office and that was what I loved it for. If I was leaving this career behind, it was nice that I'd had a little bit of time at the end to do my work quietly, surrounded by books—always my favorite place to be. I stopped in the middle of the open area. Something was different. The desk chair, now. It wasn't in the same position I had left it in, I was sure. I always pushed it in to the desk and it was not only pulled out but turned sideways.

Silly, I thought. *Must have just forgotten.* I went over to the desk and noticed some papers lying there—the one on top of the stack was the inventory list of the books bought from the Wilkes estate. I was positive I hadn't left it there. It ought to have been in the file drawer at the back of the store.

If there's one thing I have learned from watching crime dramas, it is that the plucky heroine only gets herself into trouble by exploring a building she assumes is empty to look for clues. For all I knew there was someone lurking in the bookshelves. I spun around and almost ran out of the store and back to my car. With the engine on and the doors firmly locked I got out my phone and called Todd's number. I held my breath as it rang.

"Detective Todd Mason," said his voice.

"Hi, this is Katrina. Katrina Peters. I'm at the bookstore. I think someone was in there. Maybe still is in there."

"Get out of there right now." The intensity in his voice was unnerving.

"I did. I mean, I'm out in my car now. I got scared."

"Where is your car?"

"The college parking lot."

I could hear him draw a long breath. "Ok. Sit tight till I get there."

It was only five minutes until his car pulled up alongside mine. We both got out.

"Sorry to bother you," I said. "But I didn't know what to do."

"No problem. Are you ok?" His eyes searched mine in a way that reminded me of Sheila's hero Edward. All the detachment from our previous meetings was gone.

"I'm fine," I said. "I was just rattled. And it may be nothing…"

"Why don't you explain exactly what happened?

"Ok. I unlocked the door and went in. When I saw the desk, the chair was pulled out and turned sideways. I thought that was weird because I always leave it pushed into the desk. I thought I might have just forgotten this once, but then I saw a stack of papers on the desk that I know I didn't leave there. And I turned around and came straight out."

"All right. You stay here while I go check it out."

"Here's the key," I said, handing it to him. "One of the locks is automatic when the door closes. I didn't bother with the dead bolt."

"Thanks," he said, taking the key.

"Be careful."

He grinned. "Always am."

I sat back down in my car and prayed for him. Shouldn't he have waited for backup? He came back ten minutes later. I jumped out of the car when I saw him.

"What happened?"

"It's empty now. Do you want to come with me and see if anything else is out of place?"

We walked together back to the store.

"Ok, you said your chair was in a different position

than you left it, and those papers weren't there. Anything else?"

I looked at the desk. "I don't see anything else different here." I walked around through the store, looking at all the shelves.

"Look," I said pointing. "See how these books here and there are pushed all the way in? Frank had all the spines of the books aligned with each other right at the edge of the shelf. It kept him from having to dust the front parts of the shelves. Someone took them out and then didn't align them perfectly afterwards. They're pushed in a little too far."

Todd nodded. "I can see that. Is there any reason why those particular books should be pulled out?"

I tugged several of them out all the way and looked at them. "The only thing they have in common is that they're some of the older books in the store."

"Are those the most valuable books in here?"

"Well, kind of. But they aren't that valuable. Not more than a couple hundred dollars at most. And they didn't even take them."

"They might have been looking for one particular one," said Todd.

"I wonder which one?"

Todd just shook his head. "You really need a security system."

"I'd install one if I was going to keep it, but if I end up going to PNG next year I'll probably be selling the place in a month or two, and it seems like that's something the new owner should do."

"PNG? Papua New Guinea?"

I nodded. "To teach at a mission school. But I haven't decided yet."

"I see."

He stood there looking at me for a moment. I felt like he was searching my face for some kind of clue. I began to feel awkward.

"Well, I'd better get going. I was going to do some grading and writing in here, but I feel a bit nervous about it now."

"Totally understandable. And I think we ought to go over the place for fingerprints. This is still the scene of the murder, and if someone broke in here it could be over something related to that. Nothing seems to have been taken, but I think it still merits investigation."

"I think you're right," I said. "Is there any progress on finding the stolen manuscript?"

"Some," he said. "We found out that the locks were picked."

"Is that good news or bad news?"

"Bad news in that we're probably looking at a professional criminal, which means they're going to be more careful than your average opportunistic thief. There weren't any fingerprints in the special collections room that were any help."

"Meaning that he or she wore gloves?"

"Probably so."

We walked back toward the desk. I looked at the papers without touching them. "It's odd that the inventory from the Wilkes estate should be out," I said. "Why would someone want to see what books were bought from there?"

"Unless it was someone from the Wilkes family who know that more secrets about their family might be hidden in the books that came from the old man's collection."

"True," I said. "That family seems to be up to their eyeballs in deceit. Yesterday I heard that Kelsey Wilkes is grounded for saying she was out with her cousin Matt every week when she was actually out with her boyfriend."

Todd had been looking at the spines of books on the bookshelf, but at that he turned to face me.

"Kelsey Wilkes? Are you sure?"

"Yeah. She's friends with Ed and Kim's daughter Deirdre. Kelsey couldn't come over to do her history project with Deirdre yesterday because she's grounded for saying she was out driving with her cousin Matt every Tuesday when it was really her boyfriend."

"Well," said Todd after a moment, "I think Matt's alibi for the murder has just been busted."

CHAPTER 12

All I heard in the next couple of days was that Matt had been questioned again. I assumed that if he had been arrested I would have been told, but there was really no way of knowing.

That was finals week. I was deluged under a sea of final drafts as well as the American Lit final exam. When I wasn't on campus I was at home, reading myself cross-eyed. My goal was to get everything graded by the last day of the semester. Then, I told myself, I could give my mind over completely to deciding what to do with the rest of my life.

That is not to say that certain thoughts didn't come creeping in between the ill-constructed sentences I was trying to focus on. If I did go to PNG for the school year, what would happen if I didn't like it? I would finish out the year, of course, but it was doubtful my old job as an adjunct professor would still be there for me if I moved back to the U.S. I could probably find another job at a different college, but that would mean a move, and the thought of starting over *again* in a different area was daunting.

I pulled back my wandering thoughts to the paper I was grading.

"At the age of seventeen," I read, "William Brown was arrested on one count of aggravated assault and two counts of burglary and was tired as an adult."

Tired as an adult? He probably was, with that kind of record…and then it hit me that *tired* was a typo for *tried*. I paused to copy and paste the sentence into my student bloopers file.

My phone rang. It was an unknown number.

"Hello?"

"Hi, Katrina? This is Jason Evans."

"Oh, hi, Jason. How are you?" I tried to make myself sound friendly and unconcerned. I had a suspicion that I sounded as panicked as I felt.

"Fine, thanks. I was wondering…our church is having a concert on Sunday night—it's a choir that sings a capella—and they're supposed to be really good. Would you like to come with me and Tori?"

"Sure," I said. "That sounds good."

"Great! Can we pick you up at six?"

"Sure," I said again. "I'm looking forward to it."

"Me too. See you then."

I stared into space for a minute after I hung up, wondering how I felt. Looking forward to it? Not strictly true. Or was it? Perhaps it was.

"I have a date," I said aloud. It had been a long time since I'd said that. Unquestionably it was a boost to the ego. I picked up the phone to call Kim, who I knew would kill me if I didn't report this development immediately.

"No," I said. "Finish grading first. It will be too hard to go back to it after an hour on the phone with Kim."

I put the phone down resolutely, turned my attention back to the paper, and made a note on it that William Brown had probably robbed a delicatessen, not a delicacy. Autocorrect can be a nuisance.

By Saturday morning I had finished grading everything. I loaded up my car with an umbrella, a rain jacket, bug spray, and the four giant bags of marshmallows Kim had asked me to bring and drove up to the forest in plenty of time to help set up for the Fun Day. Deirdre's art class would prevent her from coming, but the rest of the Cole family would be there. It was going to be a great day. No school to think about, no one to remind me about murders or thefts, and no potential suitors, either real or imagined. I could give my full attention to the families who were helping kids through foster care.

When I pulled into the parking lot there were already several cars there and people standing in groups. I scanned them, looking for Ed or Kim, but the only familiar face I saw was Todd's.

Wait, Todd? I looked again. Yep, there he was standing in the parking lot dressed in athletic sweats and a t-shirt—a sporty look I'd never seen on him. He was standing with a guy that looked vaguely familiar. I sat in my car and scrutinized the man, trying to place him. I finally recognized him as Detective Ortega. He seemed to be there with a wife and several kids, at least a couple of whom were a different ethnicity. He must be the foster parent Todd had mentioned on our drive into Tacoma. And Todd must have been roped in to help just like I had. There went the idea that I could serve today without distractions. Well, we would probably both be too busy to see much of each other. Maybe afterwards I could find out if anything was going on with Matt Wilkes.

I spotted the large, cheerful lady that had led the potential foster carers meeting. She had a clipboard and seemed to be in charge. June, that was her name. I went over to her and introduced myself.

"Oh, yes, Katrina! Kim said you'd be coming. You

can put whatever food you brought over there under the canopy"—she pointed vaguely toward a large striped awning with tables underneath. "That's our command center. Food, first aid, prizes and so on are all there. In about five more minutes I'll take everyone around to their challenge stations, so just sit tight."

The Coles arrived right about then, and I went over to greet them. Mia and I unloaded the boxes of burger and hot dog buns they had brought while Sam and Ben followed us with giant bags of potato chips. Out of the corner of my eye I watched Todd. I saw Ed go over to talk with him and Kim join them. I knew Ed had met Todd before because they had cleaned the carpet together, but I thought this would be Kim's first meeting with him. Before I had quite decided if I wanted her to like him or not, June had blown a whistle and motioned for everyone to come over to her. Todd saw me and waved. I waved back.

"Thank you all for coming," said June. "We have eight challenges set up, and families will all start with a different challenge so that there won't be a big delay as they wait for others to finish. Now, I'll read out the volunteers that are going to help with the challenges, and all those people come with me." She read off about sixteen names including mine and Todd's. I looked accusingly at Kim, but she shook her head and shrugged her shoulders to signify that it wasn't her doing that Todd was there. The "challenge supervisors" as June called us followed her in a disorganized mob down the trail.

The weather was beautiful. The skies were clear and the sun was hot, but under the shade of the trees the temperature was perfect. I breathed in the smell of pine and trod on the carpet of fallen fir tree needles, both sensations contributing to the familiar family-camping-trip feeling.

Every hundred yards or so there was some kind of

activity set up, and two volunteers were left there with instructions about how the challenge worked. When we got to the fourth challenge, the two names that were called out were mine and Todd's. You're not surprised, are you? Neither was I. I didn't know who was responsible, but I was certain it was not random mischance. Someone was deliberately sticking us together for the afternoon. If it wasn't Kim, it must have been Ed.

Ours was the Minefield Challenge. About twenty square yards had been roped off with yellow "caution" tape; trees, shrubs and rocks were all within the boundary. The object was for a blindfolded person to make their way around the area, picking up three small orange cones that were placed in various spots. They'd have to follow the shouted directions of their family members who would try to steer them around the obstacles, which were the "mines" to be avoided.

"Just stay here," said June to Todd and me, "and the first families will be along within about fifteen minutes. When they've completed their challenge, you give them one of these golden tickets and point them in that direction— see the orange flag tied to the tree? That's the marker they look for. When they get there, they'll see another one and it will lead them to another challenge. When all twenty tickets are gone, that will mean all the families have come through. At that point, take down the tape and pick up the cones and bring them back to the parking lot. Any questions?"

We had none, so she wished us well and trotted off with the rest of the volunteers trailing behind her. I found a handy fallen tree and sat down on it. Todd joined me.

"Nice day," he commented.

"Yeah," I said. "Good weather."

"Do you help often at these events?"

"Sometimes. Usually I help more informally, but I've helped at the Family Fun Day for the past couple years. You?"

"This is my first time helping out. John was the one who recruited me—that's Detective Ortega that you met at the station one time."

"I remember." I laughed shortly. "Actually, it would be hard to forget."

"Hard to forget John?" Todd's eyebrows rose.

"Hard to forget being suspected of murder."

"Oh, right. Yeah, I guess that would be pretty unforgettable."

"Speaking of suspects," I said, "I'm assuming that Matt wasn't arrested."

"No, not yet. We're still gathering evidence."

"I see." There didn't seem to be much more to say about that.

"I talked to your old professor again," said Todd after a moment of silence. "Dr. Weatherill. I told him about the theft of the manuscript. He seemed quite disturbed over it."

"I can imagine. He was the one who first authenticated it."

"Right. Anyway, I asked him to keep his ears open for anyone trying to sell it. And I told him about you inheriting the bookstore. He said to send you his congratulations and tell you that if you're planning to dispose of the books, he'd love to help you find buyers for them. He said he might even be interested in buying some for himself."

"That's nice," I said. "I wouldn't have thought he'd remember me." It was a cheering prospect. Evidently God was sending my old professor to help me with the sale of the books. Perhaps it was a sign about what I should do.

"I'd be shocked if he didn't remember you," said Todd. I looked at him in surprise. "You were probably a very good student," he added.

"Oh! Well, I wasn't too bad. I was hardly an amazing pupil, though. At that stage in my life I had no intention of being an English professor. I sort of fell into it later."

"What did you want to do at that point?"

"I didn't know; I wasn't really career-oriented. Mostly I just wanted to be a wife and a mother, but I thought I might as well be prepared for something in case I didn't get married. It was a good thing, as it turned out."

"Yeah, life doesn't always turn out the way you think it will." He seemed awfully serious. I wondered if he was going to talk about his failed marriage. I wasn't sure I wanted to hear it.

A noise from the path to our left intruded into our consciousness. Three laughing kids came racing up with their parents walking behind them, and for the next two hours we were busy helping one family after another to complete the challenge. I'd heard of team-building exercises but had never been part of a group that did them. Some families worked together well and others struggled more. Some of the kids lost their tempers and there was one scraped knee that needed a band-aid which Todd jogged back to the parking lot first aid station to get. I wondered if team building activities would work at the mission school; if there was a mix of missionary kids and local kids they might need some activities to unify them. Carrie would know.

When the last of the families had finished, we took the "caution" tape down and wadded it into a ball, and Todd stacked up the cones.

"Have you been all over these woods?" he asked me.

"Mostly," I said. "But I usually stick to the trails."

"Have you been down this direction?" he pointed off to the right. "There's an incredible view."

"No, I don't think I have. I'll have to see it sometime."

His eyes twinkled. "No time like the present…"

"But aren't we supposed to get back and help?"

"They have tons of help. Really."

It was true. There were almost as many volunteers as there were families, and if we were needed they could always text us.

"Ok," I said as Todd set the cones down and I put the wadded-up tape inside them. "But I feel like I'm playing hooky."

Todd laughed and started off through the trees. "You're a rule-follower, aren't you?"

I glanced at him. "Never thought a policeman would fault me for that!"

"Oh, I'm not faulting you. I think we ought to follow the rules unless the rules are causing us to break God's law. I just think sometimes rule-followers aren't following the rules because it's right but because they feel like it's safe."

"Well, that might be true of me," I conceded. "I'm not a natural risk-taker and I do like to play it safe. Do you think that's wrong?"

"I think it can be. Especially if you think following the rules will keep bad things from happening to you."

"Sometimes it does," I argued. "Think of all the verses in Proverbs that tell you that doing what is right will guard you from calamity."

"Oh, of course. And as policeman I can confirm that people who follow the laws —both God's law and the law of the land—avoid a lot of the disasters that happen to people who don't. But I'm sure you can think of a lot of godly people in the Bible that bad things happened to even though they didn't break the rules."

"That's true," I said and immediately stumbled over a rock and fell forward. I was profoundly thankful that Todd was a few steps ahead of me, because if he'd been right beside me he might have caught me. I probably would have enjoyed that, but then I would have been worried that he thought I had faked a fall for that purpose. As it was, I just looked clumsy.

"You ok?" He came back to where I was picking myself off the ground. "Sorry, I should have warned you to be careful there."

"No problem," I said. "I have eyes—I should have been looking for rocks. No harm done." I brushed my hands together and smiled as pluckily as I could.

"We're almost there. See that big rock? We're going up there."

"Oh!" It was a massive rock, fifteen feet high at least.

"It's not as bad as it looks, really. See, if we go up this way it's more of a gradual slope. I'll go first and give you a hand."

He climbed up to a ledge about five feet off the ground and reached his hand down to me. I grabbed it and let him help pull me up. I wished I was in better shape.

"Good," he said when I was beside him. "Now don't let go—there's not much climbing involved here but I don't want you to slip." He kept hold of my hand as we made our way up the rock, him leading and me trying to keep up enough that I wasn't dead weight pulling him down. When we got to the top, he let go of my hand.

"There," said Todd. "Look at that. Worth it?"

It was. We could see across a valley to the forested mountain on the other side. Far below us was a river—probably the same one that ran beside Wilkester. Birds wheeled above us in the cloudless sky.

"Breathtaking," I agreed. "'When I look down from lofty mountain grandeur…'"

"'And hear the brook and feel the gentle breeze,' added Todd. He smiled. "I thought you might quote something."

"Sorry," I said. "One of the hazards of teaching literature is that quotations are always flitting through your mind."

"Hey, it's a refreshing change from movie quotes or pop song lyrics, which is what people usually quote."

"Well, that's putting a nice spin on it." I sat down on a flat spot of the rock "I almost don't want to go back. But Kim and Ed will be out searching for me if I'm not back soon."

"Here, I'll text John to let him know where we are." Todd pulled out his phone and typed a message.

"I suspect you're a rule-follower, too," I said as he put his phone back in his pocket and sat down next to me.

"Pretty much. I think it's more often for the right reasons now, though."

"Oh?"

He nodded. We sat there silently for a little while and then he took a deep breath and said, "I told you I was married before."

I suddenly felt like I couldn't breathe. "Yes," I squeaked.

"I followed all the rules. I did everything I knew to do to be a good husband. I thought we had a good marriage. I thought we would never have problems because I was doing the right things."

I had no idea what to say. "How long were you married?" I ventured.

"Three years. I was an elder at the church—it's a church in Seattle—and she and I went to visit some of our missionaries in India."

I nodded. "Yes, you told me about going there."

"When we came back, she told me she was leaving me."

"But why?"

"She just said she couldn't do the marriage thing anymore. She walked away from God, from the church, from all our friends…and from me, obviously. No real reason. She said I didn't do anything wrong, but she just needed to be out of the marriage."

"That's horrible!" No other words came to mind.

Todd sat looking out across the valley. "It was totally devastating. Nothing in my Christian experience had prepared me for that."

"What did you do?"

"There wasn't much I could do. I begged her to stay, but she left anyway and filed for divorce. She went through church discipline—she didn't care. I stepped down from being an elder. I ended up leaving the church…not because I had to, but because it was so painful to be there around all the people who had loved us and seen us married, the girls she had been in a discipleship relationship with—all of it."

"I can imagine." I said. "How long ago was that?"

"Seven years."

"And all that time you've been hoping she would come back?"

"Oh, no. After a couple years she married someone else. Neither of them claim to be Christians."

He was silent for a while, so I decided to prompt him.

"When I met you I asked what church you go to, and you said several different ones."

"Yeah. I had a few bad experiences in the beginning when I was visiting churches. People were friendly at first and then they found out I was divorced and their attitude changed. In some ways I couldn't blame them—I probably would have done the same thing, before. Especially if it was a man who was divorced, I would have assumed he'd done something wrong, probably very wrong, that caused the problem. But that didn't really make it easier to deal with. I got into the habit of just going to the worship service at a few different churches and not getting involved in any fellowship groups or committing to any one church."

"Oh." I felt wretched. I had assumed all the same things as those people. I couldn't blame him for not committing to a church right away. In fact, I was impressed that he hadn't just stayed home.

"But I've come to realize, especially talking to your friend Ed, that I need to remedy that. He thinks your church might be a good fit for me."

"There are wonderful people there," I said. "I love it. But I can't guarantee that no one will say something hurtful."

"I know, but it's a risk I have to take."

"True." I was thinking about the risk in going to PNG and abandoning any faint prospect of ever teaching college again. Maybe that was a risk I had to take.

"We'd probably better get back," said Todd, standing up and offering me a hand to do the same.

"Yeah," I said. "We don't want to miss those marshmallows." That came out more flippantly than I had meant it to. The poor guy had just spilled his guts to me and here I was acting like we'd been talking about baseball or something. "Sorry," I said.

"For what?"

"For probably saying the wrong thing just then."

He grinned and I relaxed. "You didn't say the wrong thing. I really don't want to miss the marshmallows. We just need to go pick up those cones where we left them and then we can eat."

We didn't talk much on the way back to where the food was being barbequed, but I felt like we had shared something important. He just needed some fellowship, poor man, and I was glad I had been there to listen without condemning. I was also glad I hadn't had the opportunity to say anything about his divorce to him before—with my previous assumptions it would no doubt have been something hurtful.

Mia and Ben spotted me before I got to the tables of food and rushed up to show me their prize—they had gotten one of the homemade cookie mixes in a jar.

"And you know what we're having after the hot dogs?" said Mia. "S'mores!"

"Hey, Todd!" called a voice, and we both turned to see John Ortega waving Todd over toward his family.

"See you later," Todd said to me before moving off toward his friend.

I could see that Kim was bursting with questions for me, but she was forced to hold off while she was surrounded by her kids clamoring for help with roasting their marshmallows. I helped where I could and then tried to make up for my lack of help earlier by cleaning up as much as I could. The Family Fun Day was winding down, and the sugar-intoxicated kids were starting to get crabby. Their parents began packing up.

"*Call me*," Kim told me as she herded her kids toward their minivan. "I mean it!"

"I will," I said. I watched them drive away and then turned to find Todd right behind me.

"I meant to ask you," he said, "Do you remember telling me that you were reading that book by Thomas Watson?"

"*All Things for Good*? Yeah."

"I was wondering if I could borrow it from you—if you're finished with it, I mean. I'd like to read it again."

"Sure, no problem. You can stop by my place and get it on your way home, if you want. You probably drive almost right past my apartment. You can follow me there."

"Thanks," he said. "I'd like that."

We drove down the mountain a half-hour later. As his silver car followed mine down the curving road I faced one of my annoying dilemmas: should I invite him in and risk looking forward or just run in and get the book for him and risk looking inhospitable?

In the end I didn't have to decide. I pulled into my parking space and Todd parked nearby on the street. I walked over to his car, but as soon as he had rolled down his window to talk to me, his phone rang.

"I'll just run in and get the book for you," I said, and he nodded as he answered his phone.

I went up the stairs to my apartment, unlocked the door, and opened it.

Total chaos met my eyes. Things were turned over, drawers were pulled out, and books were thrown on the floor. I stood in the middle of the living room and gaped at the mess. There was a sound behind me. It was the last thing I heard before something hit my head and everything went black.

CHAPTER 13

"Katrina."

Someone was calling my name.

"Katrina, can you hear me?"

My head hurt like it never had before, and I couldn't open my eyes. I tried to talk but it came out as a moan.

"It's ok." The voice sounded relieved. "Everything will be ok. Just lie there. The ambulance is on the way."

That woke me up a little more. "No," I whispered. "My insurance won't pay…"

The voice chuckled. "Forget about it. I'll pay for it if I need to."

I wondered who it was. Their voice was familiar, but it didn't seem to be my dad. I couldn't think of anyone else. It was easier to rest and keep my eyes closed. I drifted off once more.

When I woke up again I opened my eyes long enough to see that I was in a hospital room and that Kim was sitting in a chair beside my bed, but the light was too bright and I shut them again.

"Kim?" I said softly.

"You're awake again! Oh, good. I'm supposed to tell the nurse." I heard her click something.

"It's so bright in here," I said. "It's hard to keep my eyes open. And my head hurts."

"Here, I have something that will help." I heard Kim fumble in her bag. "It's sunglasses," she explained. "I'll help you." I felt the glasses slide onto my face and opened my eyes again.

"That's better," I said. "What happened?"

"You got knocked out. Do you remember that?"

I shook my head and regretted it.

"I remember driving down the mountain but that's it. Did I crash?"

"No. You got home and went into your apartment to get a book for Todd, but you didn't come out again. Todd waited a few minutes before coming to see if you'd forgotten. He found the door ajar and your apartment trashed and you knocked out on the floor."

"Oh, a burglary? I was warned about that, I think. In a paper."

"What?"

"There was something about a burglary in a paper. And being tired. I think I was being warned." I paused. "No, I'm confused. That doesn't make sense."

She patted my shoulder. "It's ok. The doctor says you have a concussion. It may take a while before you're totally back to normal."

"I have to get to class! Kim, how can I teach like this?"

"Semester's over, remember? No more teaching for a while."

"Oh, right. Right." There seemed to be something else I was supposed to do, but I couldn't think what it was.

The nurse came in then and did all the nursey things—took my blood pressure and temperature and looked into my eyes with a light. I nearly cried out at the pain that caused.

"You have a concussion!" announced the nurse, as

cheerfully as if she were declaring I'd given birth to twins. "Just keep quiet, and the doctor will be in to look at you soon."

She bustled out again. I looked toward the window of the room; the light outside was dim.

"What time is it?"

"Seven in the evening. You've been here for a couple hours. Todd called me as soon as the ambulance came for you. He didn't want you to wake up in the hospital alone."

"That was nice of him."

"He told me he would have come himself, but he needed to follow up on the incident."

"Yeah, he told me once that the first few hours after a crime are the most important. Only he was talking about murder then."

"Well, this could have been a murder. He said a blow like that on the head might have killed you."

"'Mortal dangers around me fly, 'till He bids, I cannot die,'" I said.

Kim laughed. "There can't be too much wrong with you if you can still quote poetry."

"On the contrary," I said, closing my eyes. "that will be the last of my faculties to be lost."

The doctor, when he came, told me that I was very lucky I wasn't more seriously injured, and also that I must keep quiet for a while. This command was repeated by every nurse who came into the room all evening, which made me wonder: did I *look* like someone who was likely to get up and start breakdancing? I was told I would need to stay in the hospital at least overnight for observation. Kim went home at nine o'clock and I braced myself for a sleepless night. I half wished I had *Romola* with me to finish reading, except that I was pretty sure reading would have made my head throb even more. It turned out that I fell asleep almost at once and didn't wake up until the morning.

My head ached less the next day, and light in my eyes wasn't quite so painful. I tried to read a book I picked off a book trolley wheeled around by a hospital volunteer, but it quickly became clear that it was not an activity I was yet ready for. That was pretty horrifying. I've never not been able to read. I tried to pray but found it hard to concentrate. I ended up just lying there with my eyes closed for a long time.

Visiting hours in the afternoon brought Kim, holding a giant bouquet of flowers.

"Wow," I said. "You really shouldn't have. I know how much those things cost."

"I didn't buy them," she said guiltily. "These were at the front of the church this morning. Did you know they always donate them after the service to someone who's in the hospital?"

"No, but it's a good idea. They do brighten the place up."

"How are you feeling today?"

"Not too bad, but I'm still not much good for conversation. I seem to get confused easily. In fact, I don't know if I'll be able to drive home."

"You can't anyway," said Kim. "For one thing, your car isn't here, and for another, I'm sure you aren't supposed to be driving until you're a lot better."

"I can't just stay here for days on end!" I said.

"No, and you don't need to. I thought of bringing you to our house for a few days, but it's hardly quiet there and you wouldn't have your own room. But Becky said to tell you she'd love to have you at her place. It's completely quiet and she's got that spare room. She's still teaching during the day, but she's there in the evening."

"Oh, that would be perfect! I was thinking about

everything this morning and I remember going into my apartment and I thought it was really messy. Is that right?"

"Yep. Todd said someone trashed the apartment."

"I don't really feel well enough to clean it up right now."

"No, and it's a crime scene, or it was."

"Another one." My hand plucked restlessly at the hospital blanket lying over my legs. "Kim, why am I suddenly involved in all these crimes?"

"Todd thinks they're probably connected."

"You talked to him?"

Kim smiled. "He called me last night after I left you—wanted to know how you were. He said he'd be coming in today to ask you some questions."

"Oh?"

"I'd say he was *quite concerned*," she added archly. "I won't ask you a lot of questions now, but I haven't forgotten that you said you would call me and fill me in."

"I did?"

"Well, I said 'call me' and you said you would, which means the same thing. You and Todd were absent for a long time on that mountain and I need some details."

It came back to me then—sitting on that rock with Todd and talking about his marriage. The sympathy I'd felt came back, too.

A gentle knock on the door interrupted my thoughts.

"Come in," called Kim, and the door opened to reveal Todd standing there.

"Is it ok to come in and chat for a few minutes?" he asked.

"Sure," said Kim. "I'll go take a little walk so you can talk about the case." She offered her seat to Todd and he thanked her.

"Hi Katrina," he said as the door shut behind Kim.

"How are you feeling?"

"Ok," I said. "Not back to normal but a lot better than last night."

"You look a lot better. Are you up to answering a few questions?"

"I'll try."

"Thanks," he said, flipping open his notebook and getting out a pen. "First of all, did you see who attacked you?"

"I don't think so. It's all a little hazy, but I think I went into my apartment and it was messed up. I don't remember anything after that. Maybe someone hit me from behind?"

"It's very possible."

"Why do you think they wanted to hurt me?"

"My guess is that you surprised them while they were looking for something. Do you have anything valuable at your apartment?"

"No, not really. I don't have any expensive jewelry or electronics or anything—I can't imagine what they would want."

"It seems like either they were looking for something specific or they were just trashing your apartment to harass you. Do you know if anyone is upset with you? A student with a bad grade, maybe, who is unstable?"

"I can't think of anyone, I said. "The only people who might not be happy with me right now are the Wilkes family. I wrote them a letter a couple days ago saying that I was going to donate Matthew Wilkes' journal to the Wilkester Museum. I thought I ought to tell them first, in case they wanted to make an announcement about the story before the museum did. I thought they might hate me for that, but I didn't really expect to be attacked."

"Ok, we'll look into that." He wrote in his notebook

181

for a minute.

I sighed. "I'm sorry I didn't see who it was. Or if I did, that I can't remember."

"Hey," he lowered his notebook and looked into my eyes. "You are in no way at fault or responsible for any of this. You understand? Don't feel guilty."

"I'll try not to."

"There is actually a security camera out of the back of the apartment building, which is the way the intruder probably left. I didn't see anyone come out the front when I was sitting there in my car waiting for you. We're in the process of getting access to that footage now. Hopefully we'll be able to get a glimpse of whoever it was."

"That's good," I said.

He closed his notebook and stood up. He took my hand, almost as if he was going to shake it, but he just stood there holding it for a minute.

"I wish I could stay longer and chat, but I need to get back and see if we can view the security camera footage. Is there anything you need?"

"I wish I had my phone," I said. "It was in my purse, which is probably back at the apartment."

"I can get that for you," said Todd. "I'll have someone drop it off here as soon as I can."

"I might be getting released today."

"Nope, not yet," said Todd. "I just talked to the doctor and he says you can go home tomorrow if all goes well, but he doesn't want to leave you to your own devices just yet."

"Oh. Well, I guess that will give Becky more time to get ready for me—that's my friend that I'm going to stay with for a few days."

"I'm relieved to hear you won't be staying alone right away. That's a wise move."

"It was Kim's idea. She thought their place would be too noisy for me and asked Becky if I could stay with her. Besides, I don't feel up to cleaning up my apartment yet."

"I can imagine."

The door opened slightly.

"Hello!" Kim's grinning face popped in the door. Todd put my hand down. "I just came to say I have to go now—Josh needs the car to go to a concert tonight, but I'll be back tomorrow."

I gasped. "Concert! That's what I was trying to remember."

"Jason?" said Kim, cryptically, with a glance at Todd. "You want me to call him?"

"Please," I said. "I have no phone. Tell him I'm sorry."

"I don't think he'll be offended," said Kim drily.

"Don't forget," I said.

"I'll call him now," she said. "See you tomorrow. Bye, Todd."

"Bye," he echoed.

He was silent for a minute after the door closed.

"Is it nosey if I ask who Jason is?"

"Oh, just a—a friend."

He smiled a little. "A friend you had a date with?"

"Kind of. I mean, I was going with him and his daughter to a church concert. That's all."

"I see," he said. I thought he looked like he wanted to ask another question, but after a minute he only said, "Well, I need to get going. I'll see if I can get you your phone."

"Thanks a lot," I said. "Be careful."

"I always am," he said, and the last sight I had of him was that charming smile going out the door.

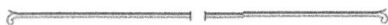

"This is your room," said Becky as she showed me into her guest room. "Sorry it's so juvenile."

I laughed. The bed had a teddy bear quilt on top of it and there were shelves filled with toys along the wall.

"I was just so excited about getting a foster child or two I couldn't wait to start getting ready."

"Not a problem," I said. "It's a lovely room. So much nicer than being in a hospital! I was brought my purse and my phone at the hospital last night, but I probably should go to my apartment and get some clothes, too."

"Oh, I forgot to tell you! Kim and Deirdre went to your place last night and packed a suitcase full of your clothes and toiletries. They're in the living room." She disappeared for a moment and returned pulling a wheeled suitcase behind her. "There. And later on I can drive you to your place so you can get anything else you need. Kim said she and Deirdre cleaned up as much as they could, so it shouldn't be too bad in there."

"Never, ever could I get better friends than you guys," I said. "I'm so blessed."

"Kim said that if you started going on and on about how grateful you were that I should remind you that you owe her information about someone named Todd."

I blushed.

"Aha!" Becky said. "Well, I figure you owe me something, too, right? For letting you stay here and feeding you and everything?"

"All right, all right," I said. "But maybe after dinner."

"I'm going to hold you to that. Dinner should be ready in about an hour, is that ok?"

"That's great. I'll probably just lie down and rest until then. I've been lying down and resting so much. I can't believe I'm still tired."

"It's what your body needs," said Becky.

I had only been lying down for ten minutes when I heard Becky's doorbell ring. The sound of muffled voices filtered through the bedroom door, and in a minute there was a soft knock on my door.

"Katrina? There's a detective here to see you."

"All right." I got up, still a little unsteady on my feet at first.

Becky was smiling when I opened the door of the bedroom and she whispered, "I think he said his name was Todd." I gave her a weak smile and went into her living room. Sure enough, there was Todd.

"I'll…uh…just go finish making dinner," said Becky, and slunk into the kitchen.

"I hope it's ok that I just dropped in," said Todd, seating himself on the sofa and motioning for me to do the same. "I had something I needed to show you."

He pulled a black and white photograph out of his shirt pocket and gave it to me. It showed a man from above and behind him; all I could really see was a dark knit hat, some light hair and a dark hoodie.

"Obviously this isn't much, but we think this is the guy that attacked you. I don't suppose you recognize the clothes? Or anything about him?"

I shook my head. "It doesn't look familiar. I'm sorry."

"Don't worry about it. We're circulating this picture around all the gas stations and small stores in your area to see if anyone remembers him coming in that day. If anyone remembers him, they might have security camera footage that would show his face."

"Oh, that's a good idea," I said, and then laughed feebly. "I'm sure the police department would be encouraged to know that I think standard police procedure is a good idea."

"They probably would, actually." Todd took the picture back and slid it into his pocket. He rested his elbows on his knees and folded his hands together. "I'm sure you must think by now that we're pretty inept, and me especially—"

"What?" I said. "I wasn't thinking that."

He looked up. "I wouldn't blame you if you did, honestly. You've been involved in several crimes—the murder, the manuscript theft, your store being broken into, someone breaking into your house and attacking you… and none of them are solved. And for the last one, I was even *parked outside your house* and I couldn't stop it."

"Oh." I'd never thought about it like that. "But I'm sure you're doing your best. Really. I know that there aren't very many clues."

"True, there aren't, and it's really unusual. Most criminals aren't masterminds and they leave a lot of evidence behind them. I solve—I mean, *we* solve a lot of cases very quickly."

"I'm sure you do." I was afraid that sounded patronising, but it was the truth.

He looked at me a little shamefacedly. "I keep wishing you'd observed me working on my last few cases. I was a lot more impressive then."

"How about coffee?" Becky's voice broke into our conversation from the kitchen. She appeared at the living room door. "Would you guys like some coffee?"

"Uh, no. No, I have to get going," said Todd. "Thanks anyway." He stood to go.

"Thanks for coming," I said. "I really do appreciate all you're doing. And I *do* think you're doing a good job."

He smiled faintly. "Thanks, Katrina. It's really good

to see you out of the hospital."

He said goodbye to both of us, and Becky opened the door for him. When she shut it again she leaned back against it and said. "I can see why Kim wanted details."

"He just came to discuss the case," I said. "He had a picture of a suspect to show me."

"It's not that. It was the way he looked at you."

"And how did he look at me?"

She shook her head. "I'll just say this: I've married off three roommates so far. I've seen that look before."

CHAPTER 14

Three days went by slowly. I rested a lot in a darkened room, ate Becky's food at regular intervals, and had nice long chats with her in the evening. Todd called once to tell me they had found footage of my attacker at a convenience store. They were trying facial recognition with known criminals to see if they could get a match, although it might take a few days.

On Friday I woke up feeling so much better that I thought I probably should be moving back to my apartment before too long. I was beginning to feel like a leech. While I will never be in danger of working myself to death, my conscience begins to bother me if I do nothing for too many days in a row. I mentioned this to Becky as she was eating a bowl of cereal before she left for school. She's one of those people that rises from bed looking perfectly put together, even in pajamas. If her hair isn't perfect, at least it has the adorably messy look that women in movies have when they wake up. My morning reflection in the mirror reminds me more of those pictures of refugees you see on the news.

"Well, don't hurry away," Becky said. "I like having the company. Besides, I think you ought to wait at least until you can drive again. That won't be for a few more days if you follow the doctor's orders."

"All right, but you've got to let me fix dinner for you tonight. I'll be here all day with nothing to do."

"Well, if you'd really like to, you can. Raid the fridge and freezer—there's plenty of stuff there. You can use whatever you want."

"Good. And maybe after you get home we could go get my laptop. Kim said she saw it in the apartment."

"Oh, I can get it for you on my way home from work, if that's ok with you. I have to run a couple errands anyway. I need a few Frisbees for a game I'm playing with the class tomorrow."

"Don't bother," I said. "I have some in my car—at least five of them. I got them one time for a game thing the Coles' were doing with some other families and I've just kept them in the trunk for outings with kids at the park. Actually, you can bring that whole crate here. I should be going through the stuff that's in there anyway, and I ought to at least look at those books that have been sitting in my trunk for the last few weeks."

"Thanks! That will save some hassle."

I pottered around for a little while after she left. Reading was still hard for me, so I listened to a Bible app on my phone. Then I got dressed, searched Becky's fridge, and made a plan for dinner: beef stew. Stew is better if it simmers all day, so I browned the chunks of beef right away with some onions and got out the potatoes and carrots to chop. I found a cutting board and potato peeler and set to work. As the pile of brown potato peels grew my mind wandered back to the subject I had set myself to ponder this week: *Should I go to PNG?* That was the first question to consider. If I got the answer to that one, the other questions would be easier. So, what about it?

There was definitely a need at the mission school that I could fill. On the other hand there were lots of needs that

I could fill all over the world. Just because I could be useful someplace didn't mean I was necessarily supposed to go there. I would leave behind an awful lot if I were to go. I'd miss my church so much. And the Coles. And Becky, and a lot of other people that I saw every week. And Todd.

Todd… Becky's words yesterday came back to me: "it was the way he looked at you." I felt myself blushing to think of it, even though no one else was there. *If* it was true that Todd wanted to see if we could make a life together, should I really go away before we could find out?

I finished the potatoes and started in on the carrots. Becky and Kim both thought Todd was interested in me, but the fact remained that he hadn't said anything. *And can you blame him?* said the voice in my head. *You know how afraid you were to date again after Brian broke up with you all those years ago, and that was a very mild and brief sort of romance. Imagine if you had been married to him?*

"Very true," I said aloud. I tried to remember anything else he had ever said about love or marriage, other than his revelation on that rock. It was difficult to recall much conversation about anything except the aspects of the cases we were involved in. And foster care. And the book club.

"Number Fourteen!" I exclaimed. He had told me it was his favorite of the Elizabeth Barrett Browning poems he'd read for the book club meeting. I tossed the chopped carrots and potatoes into the stew pot with the meat, added some water and some beef broth, put the lid on, and set the pot on a low heat. Then I reached for my phone to look up Sonnet Fourteen.

> If thou must love me, let it be for nought
> Except for love's sake only. Do not say
> "I love her for her smile—her look—her way

Of speaking gently,—for a trick of thought
That falls in well with mine, and certes brought
A sense of pleasant ease on such a day"—
For these things in themselves, Belovëd, may
Be changed, or change for thee,—and love, so
wrought,
May be unwrought so. Neither love me for
Thine own dear pity's wiping my cheeks dry,—
A creature might forget to weep, who bore
Thy comfort long, and lose thy love thereby!
But love me for love's sake, that evermore
Thou may'st love on, through love's eternity.

Yes, I could understand why he liked that one. It would be more accurate, I thought, if one could change it to say, "but love me for Love's sake"—Love meaning God, because God is love. If one loves for God's sake, the love will not change even if the object of the love does. I wondered if he had read it that way.

And then there was Jason. I hadn't even decided if I could like him as more than a friend. Oddly, that question hadn't come up with Todd. In the words of Harriet Vane, "if I once gave way to Peter, I should go up like straw." I'd been holding myself back from liking him, but I doubted that anyone, even Todd, had any misgivings about whether or not I could be in love with him. "That," as Miss de Vine said drily to Harriet, "is moderately obvious." It's irritating to be so transparent.

I looked at the clock. Time for a sandwich. I had thought I could make some homemade rolls to go with the stew, but I was getting exhausted and probably needed to take a nap. That's another thing movies get wrong, I decided. They always seem to have the hero get knocked out and be unconscious for hours and then wake up and immediately fight his way out of a guarded building.

I slept longer than I intended to, only waking when Becky came back with my laptop and my crate of stuff.

"Mmm, that soup smells great!" she said. "Do you mind if we eat before we deal with your stuff? I'm starving."

"No problem. I'm hungry, too"

When we'd finished eating and doing the dishes, we repaired to the living room.

"Here's the crate," she said. "Do you mind if I look at those old books? I've been eying them for the past couple hours."

"Go ahead," I said. I dug through the rest of the clutter in the crate to get to the Frisbees—the manual for a car I used to own, a ratty sweatshirt, two outdated college brochures, a rope used for tying something to the roof…

"This is so cool," said Becky. *"The Collected Wit and Ballads of the Peasants of Many Lands*. I can't even find a date of publication on it."

I put down the old church bulletin I was looking at and peered over at the book that was sitting open on her lap. "Let's see what I can tell you about it. For one thing, it's quarto size."

"What does that mean?"

"Well, paper was produced in giant sheets that were printed and folded into different sizes. If the big sheet of paper was folded in half and bound together, it was a folio; if it was folded and then cut into fours, it was a quarto; eight folds and it was an octavo. Most quarto books were about nine inches by twelve inches, like this one is."

"It has f's instead of s's sometimes. I've always wondered why they did that. I mean, there are actual s's as well. Why didn't they just use all regular s's? Did they not have enough?"

"Yeah, it's a little confusing. The short answer is that

the medieval scribes had a long s that was used in certain circumstances, like the first of two s's that came together and at the beginning of words. When type was invented, they carried over that long s to print, but there was also an abbreviated long s that looked a lot like an f."

"It makes it really hard to read," said Becky. "It looks like it says 'for the pleafure of perfons in the prefent and times to come, so that none may be loft…' It would take me ages to figure out what they were trying to say."

"You have to get used to it," I said. "After a while you automatically see it as an s in your mind and it doesn't bother you. Oh, and here's another little thing that shows how old it is: see how whenever there's a c and a t together or an s and a t together, there's a little arc connecting them? That's also leftover from medieval scribes. It got dropped somewhere in the seventeen hundreds. I'd say this book was printed somewhere between the late sixteen and early seventeen hundreds."

"Wow," said Becky. I don't think I've ever held anything that was quite this old before."

She studied the title page which sported a rather ugly woodcut of a peasant woman and tried to read the words underneath it. I looked at the page again. There was something familiar about it, even though I was pretty sure I hadn't seen it before.

"The water stains," I said suddenly. "It has water stains like the Bradstreet manuscript. Let me see that." I took the book into my own hands and looked at it more closely. Then I turned a page. The water stains were exactly in the same place and in the same pattern as those on the Bradstreet manuscript. Illumination was dawning in my mind. I turned to the flyleaf that should have been there— the blank page between the hard cover and frontispiece.

"It's gone," I whispered. "Someone cut it out." Part

of the mystery was solved.

Two hours later, Todd sat on Becky's couch examining the book.

"Let me get this straight," he said. "You're telling me that the Bradstreet manuscript that was stolen was also a forgery?"

"That's right."

"And what happened to the original, then?"

"There probably wasn't one," I said. "At least not since Anne Bradstreet sent hers off to the printer. The originals were all lost, just like everyone thought they were for several hundred years."

"And you're saying that the manuscript the library had for years was manufactured relatively recently?"

"I think so," I said. "I think what happened was that someone who was very knowledgeable came across this book at some point. They knew that the paper would be the correct era, and they took out the flyleaf to use as the basis of a forged manuscript. Why they chose Anne Bradstreet to copy, I'm not sure, except that she was an easy poet to forge, since we have no examples of her penmanship. Interest in her work certainly revived in the twentieth century with the rise of feminism, so I doubt anyone forged her work earlier than that."

"So you think this book once belonged to the forger?"

"Either that or he had access to it without a lot of supervision."

"And he cut out the empty page and created the manuscript which eventually ended up at that university."

"Right. It's been done before—most notably by

someone in the nineteenth century that tried to forge things from Robert Burns. He wasn't very successful because he wasn't good at copying Burns's writing—we have lots of examples of it to compare fakes to—but the paper he used was fine."

"That makes sense. Now, where did this book come from?"

"It was one of those that you found at Frank's house and gave to me at the police station one day."

"And you don't think Frank was the forger." Todd said it as a statement rather than a question.

"Not for a minute. I think he opened the book and saw the resemblance to the manuscript and knew something was fishy. I also think he wanted to be sure about it before he said anything. He knew what a blow it would be to the college to have it exposed as a fake. I think that's why he was asking me about forgeries and emailed Professor Weatherill."

"The question is, where did he get this book, and when?"

"I'm not sure, but the most recent shipment we got was from the estate of old Mr. Wilkes, who died recently."

"The book list that was out on the desk in your store when you found out someone had been in there—was that from the Wilkes estate?"

"Yes! That's right. What if someone was looking for this book?"

"And when they couldn't find it there, they went to your house to look for it."

"Ohhhh. And they couldn't find it at either place because it was in my car the whole time."

Todd looked puzzled. "In your car?"

"Yeah. I...uh...put it in there—put the whole stack in there—when you gave it to me at the station and then just kept forgetting to take them out." There went any chance Todd might think me efficient and organized. He took this revelation without any noticeable shock.

"I see. Well, I doubt whoever was looking for it would think to search your car."

"I wonder why they didn't look at Frank's house."

"They probably did. We can check for signs of that. But no one is living there right now, and chances are the would-be thief could take his time to search without ripping things apart. Probably no one would ever have known."

I sighed and leaned back on the sofa. "Then why steal the forged Bradstreet manuscript?"

"My guess is that the forger, or maybe an associate of the forger, found out that Frank—or someone else—was wise to the fraud. They thought that if they could keep anyone from re-examining the manuscript, there would be no way to prove it was a fake."

"Do you think that's who killed Frank?"

"It's the best motive we've come across yet."

"But if the manuscript was gone, why try to get the book as well?"

"Either there's something about the book that would lead us to the forger or else the forger was just trying to be doubly safe. It would be very hard to prove a fraud if both the manuscript and the book it came from vanished."

"I can see that," I said. "So what is the next step?"

"We need to find out if old Mr. Wilkes told anyone about this book. We'll try to trace where he got the book from in the first place, although that might be difficult. We'll have to look into his death, too. He might have been killed to keep him quiet and everyone assumed he died of natural causes. And we'll need to see if Frank told anyone, too."

"In that email he wrote to Professor Weatherill he

said he hadn't told anyone."

"So he said, but we can't be sure. And he might have told someone after he wrote the email. He mentioned it to you, after all. We also need to see if whoever donated the manuscript to the college knew it was a forgery or collected it in good faith. And find out where he got it from."

"You mean checking auction house records?"

"Probably. Is that how collectors get their books?"

"Sometimes. But there are also book dealers that keep an eye out for items that they know their clients would like."

Todd looked at his watch. "I'd better get going. We have a lot of new leads to pursue. I'm going to have to keep the book at the police station as evidence."

"Sure. Any luck with the security camera footage?"

"Some. Facial recognition matched a couple different people who had police records, so we're following up on that."

"It wasn't Matt Wilkes, then?"

"No. He was actually at work at the time. We can't rule him out for some other things, but he isn't the person that attacked you."

"Good."

Todd was at the front door, but he turned around to face me. "And Katrina—"

"Oh, are you leaving, Todd?" said Becky, coming into the room. "I was about to offer you coffee, but I guess it's too late now."

He smiled at her. "Yes, sorry. I need to get going. Next time." He opened the door to leave.

"Were you going to tell me something?" I said.

"Yes. Yes, I was going to tell you something." He swung the door almost closed again. "I wanted to tell you to be careful. Don't tell anyone about finding the book or what you suspect about the manuscript being a forgery. We don't know who it is that is so desperate that the facts not be known, so just don't talk to anyone about it."

"That will be easy," I said. "I'm not talking to anyone anyway."

"You're getting better all the time, and it won't be long until you're interacting with people from the college and talking to people about the bookstore. Just don't say any more about anything that isn't already public knowledge. Ok?"

"Ok."

"Thanks." He patted me briefly on the shoulder and went out the door. I stood there absentmindedly and watched him get into his car and drive away.

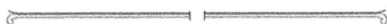

Nothing exciting happened for another week, unless you consider canceling things to be exciting. The May meeting of the book club, my involvement with Sunday School, and my reservation for the English Department end-of-the-year party were all abandoned. I felt that I had new appreciation for a whole host of characters who were incarcerated, and I toyed with the idea of changing my username for online banking to LittleDorrit. After a few more days with Becky I put my foot down, and the Coles picked me and my suitcase up and took us back to my apartment.

"Are you *sure* you're going to be ok now?" Kim asked for the fourth time.

"Yes, I'm sure. It's been two weeks, and though I'm not totally back to normal, as long as I get plenty of rest and don't overdo things, I'm good."

"Well, we stocked your fridge and cleaned up your

apartment as much as we could. I'm sure some things got put in the wrong places, though."

"You stocked my fridge?" I remembered what had happened the last time someone did that. They'd forgotten that a single person doesn't eat nearly as much as a family and I had to give away half of the perishable items before they went bad.

"Don't worry," said Ed. "Most of it is in cans or jars or else frozen. It should last until whenever you need it. Plus, we thought convenience foods would be easier for you to fix while you're recovering."

"That's a relief. Thanks. Can you stay for a little while? I could make lemonade or something."

"Wish we could," said Kim, "But we'd better get back. Mia's not doing great right now."

"Oh? What's up?"

"Her birthmother got out of prison last month and the judge has ordered supervised visits once a month. The first one is in a couple days."

"Oh, gosh. That must be traumatic."

"Yeah. She remembers being locked in the trunk of a car for hours while her mom was getting high and doing who-knows-what to get more money for drugs."

I just shook my head. "You'd better go home. Give Mia a big hug from Aunt Katrina."

"Maybe in another week you'll be well enough to stand all our noise."

"You'd better believe it," I said. "And if you don't invite me soon, I'll just show up on your doorstep demanding food and hugs."

When they were gone, I made an exploratory trip around the neighborhood in my car. I wanted to make sure I felt safe driving before I made a longer trip. I felt a little shaky and uncertain, but I thought that if I drove a little every day, I'd soon get used to it again.

CHAPTER 15

Three days later I determined that I really needed to do something about the bookstore. I'd decided not to sell the building; at least not yet. After a lot of prayer, I was sure that God wasn't asking me to go to PNG this fall, so after sending an email to Carrie and breaking the news, the next step was to get rid of all the books in the store. I wasn't sure if I would save the money I made from the books or invest it or use it to fund a ministry (like Kim's ministry coffeehouse idea), but I could settle that later. The first step was to actually sell the books.

I realized that I needed to retrieve all the mail that had accumulated for the bookstore since the murder. Frank had had a post office box for the business, so armed with an official letter from the lawyer to say that I was now authorized to deal with those letters, I went into the post office and emerged with a grocery bag full of mail.

I took an entire afternoon to sort through it, taking breaks when I needed to. Many of them were requests for books or receipts for past transactions. One of them was actually addressed to me.

Dear Miss Peters,

I have discovered from an old friend, George

Weatherill, that you have inherited Frank's Book Store. He mentioned that he'd heard you were thinking of selling the books *en masse* instead of keeping the store going. If this is so, may I beg to look them over and make an offer for some of them? I do not know precisely which books you have, but I know that some of the collections Frank acquired were very good, although I fear not correctly valued by him.

    Cordially,
    Otis Glass

    I'd heard of Otis Glass, of course, He'd had some dealings with Frank's store before, and Frank had mentioned him a few times as a reputable dealer in old books. Mr. Glass had included his email address and telephone number on the letter, and I called him immediately. He didn't answer, but I left a voice message telling him I'd be very interested in having him look at the books and buy what he liked. With any luck, he would pay me good prices for the books that were valuable, and I might be able to sell the rest to a dealer who didn't specialize in any particular literature.

    Todd called me that evening.

    "Hey, how are you feeling?"

    "Better all the time. I drove into Wilkester today. It was nice to get out of the four walls."

    "I'll bet it was."

    "Any news on the case?"

    "Yes, a little bit, which is why I called. We found the burglar who attacked you. He's in custody now."

    "Oh, that's a relief."

    "It was worrying you?"

    "It must have been. I hadn't thought much about it, but I feel so much lighter now. Is he the one that murdered

Frank, too?"

"I'm afraid not. He says he was hired to find a book—in fact, the one with the water stains."

"So we were right!"

"Yes, apparently. The thing was, the man who hired him had the name of the book slightly wrong. He said he wasn't sure but he thought it was a very old book called *Peasant Tales from Other Lands*. And he mentioned water stains. Yateman—he's the thief—couldn't find it, of course, but that's why he pulled the old books out in your store, to check for water stains."

"So he was the one who broke into my store."

"Yes."

"Why was my apartment so trashed and the store wasn't? I didn't think it could be the same person doing both."

"That was because of timing. He searched the store in the middle of the night and ran very little risk of being caught. He knew he could take his time. With your apartment, he had no idea how long you would be gone, so he searched it the fastest way he could. When he searched Frank's house, he also had all the time in the world to do it carefully—that's why we didn't even notice."

"He seems to have confessed to a lot," I said.

"Well, he was facing a charge of attempted murder. It was in his best interest to be cooperative."

"So I guess the big question is, who hired him?"

"He doesn't know. It was all done by email with an email account that has since been deleted and an IP address that was someplace in Thailand—obviously routed that way to camouflage the identity of the sender. Our computer guys are doing what they can, but they're not holding out a lot of hope."

I stifled a sigh. I was sure the policemen were doing

everything that was humanly possible, but on TV mystery shows the computer guys can trace anyone within a few hours and come up with their bank records, work history, tax returns, photos, and favorite candy at the click of a button.

"But listen," I said. "I've been thinking. Why would someone go to so much trouble, first to create a manuscript like this, and then to cover it up? It's not like a Shakespeare folio that would be worth millions."

"I don't know, but I'm guessing that whoever is responsible has a lot more at stake than just whatever penalty they would get for forgery and fraud."

"I see."

There was a pause.

"Anything new with you?" he asked, as if he was trying to find a way to prolong the conversation.

"Other than getting out of the apartment today, not really. Oh, I did make contact with a man who wants to look through the books at the bookstore and buy some of them. He's a dealer Frank has done business with before."

"You mean you were going to meet with him at your bookstore?"

"That's the plan. I don't know how else he could see the books."

"Alone?"

"I guess so. I hadn't really thought about it. Wait, you think he could be the murderer?"

"It's possible. You know that whoever did the forgery is the main suspect for the murder, too. And we know that the forger had access to old books and a lot of knowledge about old manuscripts."

"Oh! Well, do you think I should take someone with me to meet with him?"

"I think I should be there. If you unmask a master

criminal, I want to be on hand to arrest him."

"No problem," I said. "If you want to come."

"I do. Let me know as soon as you have the meeting set up. Listen, I have to go. Take care."

He hung up before I could even say goodbye. I wondered how many cases he was investigating at the same time.

I drove myself to the Coles' for dinner the next day. I felt like a long-lost relative coming home. Everyone embraced me, even Sam and Josh, and Molly the St. Bernard gave me a slobbery kiss on my elbow. Houdini contented himself with jumping up on me and barking repeatedly until Sam took him away and put him in a crate.

The noise was a little deafening, and Kim had to remind the kids two or three times to keep their voices down. I didn't mind, though. I was in the mood for celebrating. A bit of a headache was a small price to pay. Dinner was spaghetti and meatballs with salad.

"The kids all helped to make it," said Kim.

"I cut the lettuce!" announced Mia. "Isn't it good?"

"It's just about the best lettuce I ever tasted," I said, and she beamed.

After dinner there was an argument about the best way to spend the evening. Most of the kids wanted to play a board game, but Josh and Sam wanted a video game tournament. I felt like either of those was going to be too noisy for me.

"I know!" I said. "Why don't we all walk to the park? It's such a nice evening. We could even bring the dogs. It will still be light for a couple more hours."

The novelty of the idea was enough to make the kids agree to it. Ed said he needed to stay home to work on a presentation for his department, but everyone else grabbed a jacket and Sam put leashes on the dogs. Josh took a soccer ball.

"This is nice," I said as Kim and I walked the dogs behind the kids who had run ahead of us toward the park. "Weather perfect, fellowship with friends, health restored…well, pretty much restored."

"So update me," said Kim. "Yesterday you told me about that Otis guy writing to you. Did he write back after you left the message?"

"Yep. We're meeting on Monday afternoon at the bookstore."

"And you're not going alone to meet him, right?"

"Right. A policeman will be there. Although you know they caught the guy who attacked me. He's in custody."

Kim smiled. "That policeman who will be there with you—he's not a detective by any chance?"

I rolled my eyes. "Before you start in commenting on that," I said, "Tell me how that visit with Mia's birthmother went yesterday."

Kim shuddered. "It was pretty awful, actually. I wasn't there, of course, but it was supervised by a social worker and she told me that Rhonda—that's the birthmother—told Mia she was going to bring her back home with her."

"Yikes! Can she do that?"

"Not without fulfilling a number of requirements. It would be a while before that could happen. The court has to give her a chance to get her child back, but she would have to do her part, and the social worker reminded her of that. She got upset and started saying all kinds of things, like no one had the right to keep her child from her, and she was going to get her back no matter what. Mia was pretty terrified. The social worker cut the meeting short."

"Poor Mia!"

"It's one of my nightmares," said Kim, "That an abusive birth parent will find out where we live and try to kidnap their child."

"Don't even think about it," I advised. It would be one of my nightmares, too, if I became a foster parent. I had my first serious qualm about whether or not I could actually be a foster parent and face that possibility. I wondered if I had been too hasty in deciding against going to PNG.

We had reached the park by then, and Kim and I sat on a bench and watched the kids for a long time as they played hide and seek and tag together. Ben was a remarkably good "finder" and seemed to be able to sniff out his siblings no matter where they hid...all except for Mia. I had watched her slide under the leafy branches of a bush and disappear, otherwise I might have been worried.

As daylight turned to twilight, Kim called the kids to collect their jackets and the soccer ball so we could head home. They groaned but submitted.

"I've got ice cream and strawberries at home for them," she said softly to me. "They wouldn't be so reluctant to obey if they knew what was coming."

"I suppose I'm like that, too," I said. "I'm always afraid that obeying God is going to make me miserable."

"Don't we all," Kim said.

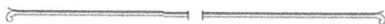

I went to church on Sunday and was greeted joyously by my troupe of pre-schoolers. I even taught the lesson about Daniel in the lion's den and made the mistake of having a contest to see which child could roar the loudest. My ears were still ringing when the service was over.

"Any news?" said Becky when the last child was

picked up.

I told her the latest about the case and was given a disgusted look in return.

"That's not the kind of news I meant," she said.

On Monday at two o'clock I met Todd outside the bookstore. He had told me not to get out of my car until he was there, so I waited until his car pulled up before opening my door. I'd wondered if we would have any time to chat, but Otis Glass's car arrived just as Todd was saying hi to me.

Otis was a small round person, chatty and cheerful and looking like the absolute antithesis of a cold-blooded murderer. Still, I've read a lot of novels where the most unlikely person turned out to be the bad guy, so it was reassuring to have Todd along. I introduced Todd simply as "my friend," which happened to be true, and thus was spared the moral dilemma faced by Christians involved in covert operations that include telling lies.

The bookstore smelled a little musty after so many weeks of disuse, and we propped the doors open to air it out a bit. Todd pulled out a book from one of the shelves and sat at the desk to read it. I gathered that he didn't think Mr. Glass was likely to pull out a gun or tip a bookshelf over on me.

"Well, this is very nice," Otis said, as he surveyed the shelves. "Quite a wide variety of books. Some people specialize—myself included—but it's amazing the treasures you find sometimes when everything is thrown together."

"True," I said, thinking of Emily Post. I *was* going to keep that one book, at least.

"Has Weatherill seen these yet?"

"No, not yet. He sent me a message saying he was interested in getting some books from me, but he hasn't contacted me directly yet."

"Ah, well, for once I've got the jump on him. Doesn't happen often, I tell you. That man knows everyone."

"I can imagine," I said. "He's been around books forever—teaching about them, buying and selling them. He was actually one of my professors at UCSC."

"That would be before he moved to Portland," nodded Glass. "He's been at North Oregon University for years now."

"Oh, is that where he is?"

"Yes. Travels all over, of course."

He ran his finger across a row of books and pulled out one by Thackeray. Unhurriedly he opened it and casually turned a few pages.

"Now this is a prize. *The Book of Snobs.*"

"Yes, that's a British edition—not a first edition, of course, but still pretty old."

"Not only that." He pointed to a signature on the flyleaf: Harriet Fuller. "You know who that is, of course."

"No, sadly, I don't."

"Thackeray's granddaughter. It was she who gave the job of writing the first authorized biography of her grandfather to Gordon Ray. This book was once in her library."

I was suitably impressed. "I don't suppose she left any original letters from her grandfather in its pages?"

"Ha ha! Yes, you're thinking of the Bradstreet manuscript, left between the pages of the family Bible. I was surprised Weatherill didn't buy that Bible when it went up for auction. He was an acquaintance of that Bradstreet descendant, you know. He's a canny fellow—scrapes an acquaintance with every descendant of famous authors that he can. He's gotten some of his best finds that way. When that descendant dies, he finds out where the books are going, and if they're for sale, he's on hand to snap them up."

"Who did buy the Bible with the Bradstreet manuscript?"

"Oh, some fellow named Boyd. Never heard of him before that. Come to think if it, haven't heard of him since. As soon as he found the manuscript he brought it to Weatherill—don't know how he knew him—and Weatherill vetted it and had it looked at by a couple other experts—protocol, you know—and he sold it on pretty quickly to a collector. That's how it ended up at the college, I believe. Donated by that collector?"

"Right," I said. "Well, I'll leave you to look over the books and see which ones you might want." I retrieved Emily Post, assured Todd that he didn't need to give up his chair, perched on top of the now-empty desk, and refreshed my knowledge of the etiquette of tea parties. It is advisable, if one is serving more than just tea, that small tables be set out for use by the guests. "In fact," Emily warns, "the hostess who, providing no individual tables, expects her guest to balance knife, fork, jam, cream cake, plate and cup and saucer, all on her knees, should choose her friends in the circus rather than in society." I laughed aloud.

"What is it?" asked Todd. He had moved the chair to the side of the desk so that he was sitting more or less beside me.

"Oh, nothing really," I said. "I just like the way she puts things." Nothing is worse than reading aloud a passage you find funny to someone else and having them try to laugh at it, too, when you know they don't see anything amusing about it. I made sure I didn't make any more noises after that.

It was an hour before Mr. Glass had finished looking through the books. He stacked them on the counter by the cash register—nearly fifty of them. I added up the prices and then gave him a discount for buying in bulk. He was so pleased that I wondered if I should have asked for more money.

We helped him carry the books out to his car—he'd brought along boxes to put them in—and then bid him goodbye. I closed the doors, turned off the lights, and locked up the store again.

"Well," I said as I stood by my car with my keys in my hand, "Do you think he was the murderer?"

"No," said Todd, "but we need to find this man Boyd who bought that Bible from the auction of the Bradstreet descendant's library. Nothing would be easier than to slip it into a book you just bought and say you discovered it there."

"I remember you telling me a couple weeks ago that one of the next steps was to trace who had bought that book. Were you not able to find out who from the auction house?"

Todd sighed. "It was on my list of things to do. I called them, but their records aren't online and I was going to have to go over their books in person—it was an auction house in Eugene, Oregon. The thing is, there's been another case that's been taking up a lot of time. In fact, I'm late for a meeting about it now."

"I'm sorry to hear it," I said. "Not because of you not having time for this case, I mean, but because you must be tired. You don't look too tired—I wasn't saying that because you look bad or anything—but I'm sure it's hard to be so busy." I bit my tongue to stop the babbling.

The charming smile flashed in my direction. "I'll survive. See you soon."

To: dr.kpeters@wilkester.edu
From: mjwilkes@wilkester.edu
Subject: Sorry

Dear Dr. Peters,

I feel that I owe you an apology for my behavior about Matthew Wilkes' journal. Do you remember me telling you that I really liked old books? That was why you sent me to Frank's Book Store in the first place. The reason I like old books is because of my great-grandfather. My mom used to bring me to his house when I was young and she would talk with him and I would look at the books. I read some of them, and some he wouldn't let me touch because they were valuable.

I don't think he ever read any of them himself, actually. He had inherited a lot of them from his father, and he had added a few himself, I think because he thought they were an investment more than anything. I remember him telling me about someone who came to assess the worth of the books and how it took him three days to catalogue all of them and figure out how much they were worth. He was really proud of having something that impressed a professor.

Anyway, I remember seeing the journal among the books, even though I didn't know what it was. I thought it was just another old book. I don't think any of my relatives knew, either. When I saw it at the bookstore, I lost my head. It seemed to me that it was personal property that belonged to the family. When I skimmed it and read the true story of what happened at the flood all those years ago, I also panicked. All I could think of was that they would pull down the statue of Matthew Wilkes in front of City Hall. As I am named for him, I felt like I would be disgraced as well.

I read the letter you wrote to my family. I'm sorry you felt so badly about letting the truth be known. I feel it was my fault, because my bad reaction to finding the book must have made you think my whole family would react the same way. And they didn't. They were surprised and unhappy that the wrong story had been perpetuated for so long, but they all agreed that to try to cover it up would be the worst thing they could do. They've been talking to the museum about some kind of joint statement they can make about the whole thing.

I just wanted to write to you and tell you not to feel bad anymore. I really did enjoy your class, and I hope I can take another class from you some time.

Sincerely,
Matt Wilkes

To: mjwilkes@wilkester.edu
From: dr.kpeters@wilkester.edu
Subject: re: Sorry

Dear Matt,

Thank you so much for your email. It relieved my mind a good deal, and I am thankful your family is choosing to be open about everything. I enjoyed having you as a student in my class, and I do hope you will be in another class of mine sometime.

By the way, you don't happen to know which expert it was that assessed your great-grandfather's books and when exactly that was? It might be very important, and I would be very grateful if you can find out.

Sincerely,
Professor Peters

It was a very long shot, but I wondered if that mysterious professor from sometime in the misty past had, while alone with old Mr.Wilkes' books, taken the opportunity to abstract the flyleaf of *The Collected Wit and Ballads of the Peasants of Many Lands.*

CHAPTER 16

On Saturday morning, just after I'd finished breakfast, my phone rang.

"Hi Katrina, it's Kim. You want to come and meet our new baby?"

"Your *what?*"

"Baby. It was an emergency placement last night. He's the sweetest thing—two weeks old and just gorgeous."

"I'll be right there." Kim knows how much I love babies.

He was absolutely adorable. Skin the color of a latte, eyes like chocolate chips and hair that was just beginning to curl. He slept in my arms peacefully while Kim and I chatted.

"His name is Amos. At least, that's the name he's going by right now. He was found outside a hospital in a cardboard box."

"Ugh," I said. "Unbelievable."

"Well, it's not as bad as you might think," Kim said. "For one thing, he was put in a place where he would get help and be found quickly. For another thing, he was well taken care of, and there were no drugs in his system. His birthmother may have just felt she couldn't take care of him and had her own reasons for not going through regular adoption channels. But he wasn't abandoned in one of those sickening ways that makes your stomach churn."

"Like in a dumpster or something," I said.

"Yeah. They'll see if they can trace his mother or any other family; she might just need some support. But until then, we get to care for him."

"Lucky you," I said, and I meant it. "How do the other kids like him?"

"They're pretty excited about him, all except Mia. I don't know if it's because she doesn't want to share the spotlight or she feels threatened or jealous or what, but she's definitely unhappy."

"I saw her playing out front with another little girl when I came up to the house."

"Yes, thank goodness her friend came over and wanted to play. It's distracted her from Amos being here."

"Well, I'm happy to hold him if you want to do something with her."

"Actually, if you don't mind holding him for a while, I'd like to start prepping some food for tonight's dinner. It's one of those recipes where there are a million things to chop up. He'll actually probably wake up and want to eat soon."

"No problem," I said.

Kim got to work in the kitchen while I dared to imagine myself as this little one's foster mother. Or even his adoptive mother. If Amos's birthmother couldn't be found, he would be able to be adopted by his foster parents. There might be another little one in the same situation for me to take care of someday.

My phone rang. I fished it out of my purse with one hand.

"Hello?"

"Hi Katrina, it's Todd."

"Oh, hi. Anything new?"

"There is, actually, and I was hoping to talk to you about it."

"No problem. I've got time. Go ahead."

"Actually, I was hoping to talk to you in person."

"Oh! That's fine too, but I'm not home right now. I'm at the Coles' house."

"Would it be all right if I went there? This is rather important."

"Sure. Do you need the address?"

"No, I know where it is. I'll be there soon."

"Hey, Kim, we're about to receive a visit from Todd," I said when I'd hung up. "I hope that's ok."

"Of course. Always happy to play chaperone," she said.

"It's about the case, my dear friend. No chaperones needed."

"Case, shmase," she retorted. "Your head is in the sand."

I was getting a little tired of everyone but Todd himself telling me that he was interested in me. Baby Amos stirred in my arms. I couldn't resist kissing his soft little forehead. His eyes opened at that.

"Amos is awake," I informed Kim.

"Oh, then I'll get his bottle ready," she said. "He hasn't eaten for three hours, and he'll probably want food." He was getting fussy by the time the bottle was prepared, and Kim let me feed him. He took a good four ounces of formula before he refused to take more, and just as I was burping him, the doorbell rang.

It was Todd, of course. Kim let him in and directed him to the family room where I was congratulating Amos on a nice loud burp.

"Hi Todd," I said.

217

"Who's this?

"This is the Coles' newest foster baby," I said.

"Hey there, Buddy," said Todd. "You sure are cute."

"I can take him now," said Kim, "so you guys can talk. Ben, can you please go get Sam and tell him that Molly needs a walk?"

"Is Molly a dog or a child?" asked Todd.

"A dog," Kim and I said together and then laughed.

"Would you mind if Katrina and I took her for the walk? I think we might have more privacy out of the house."

"Sure," said Kim. "I'll go get the leash."

"Wow, that's one big dog," said Todd when we went into the back yard and the St. Bernard got to her feet to greet us.

"But she's a sweetheart," I said, clipping the leash to her collar. "Come on, Molly!"

We went through the gate at the side of the house out to the front sidewalk. I was surprised to see a black and white police car parked on the street.

"My car's in the shop for something," Todd explained. "I'm just using the squad car for today."

"I just hope the neighborhood doesn't think the Coles are under arrest," I said, and Todd laughed.

"Maybe I should have parked farther down the street."

We walked in silence for a minute. It was all very…domestic, that was the word, walking a dog with Todd. But it wasn't why he was here, of course.

"So, what is it you wanted to tell me?"

"A couple things. The first one is that we found out about the man who bought the Bible from the Bradstreet descendant—the one who found the poem manuscript between the pages."

"Boyd? The one Otis Glass mentioned?"

"Yes. Phillip Boyd. We had to do a lot of digging, but we finally figured out who he was."

"And did you talk to him?"

"No. He died about two weeks ago."

"Of what?"

"Hit and run."

"No! Really?"

"Really. And if you think it sounds like too much of a coincidence, so do I. I was able to talk to his wife and ask her about why he bought the Bible and a few other books from that auction."

"He wasn't a collector?"

"No. His wife says he bought the books as a favor for a friend who didn't want his name to appear in the auction records. She didn't know why, and she's not sure her husband knew, either. This friend had given Boyd the money and told him which books he wanted, and Boyd had done the buying."

"That sounds suspicious," I put in.

"It's even more suspicious when you find out that Boyd and his friend found the manuscript poem in the Bible together and Boyd had thought it was lucky that his friend knew a lot about old books and could authenticate it."

I stopped walking. "*Professor Weatherill?*"

Todd nodded. "Phillip told his wife that he'd wondered if everything was above board. He thought it was odd that after the manuscript was discovered, his friend wanted him to appear as the seller to some book collector, instead of selling it on under his own name. But when other experts had looked at it too, and thought that it was genuine, he decided he must have been wrong. That was all she knew about it."

Molly began tugging on the leash, and I started moving again.

"How did he know Weatherill?"

"He was Weatherill's accountant before he—Boyd, I mean—moved to Oregon. The Bradstreet descendant lived in Oregon too, and Weatherill used to visit him. When the descendant died and the library was put up for auction, he must have recalled that Boyd lived near Eugene and asked him to buy the books on his behalf."

"But it's unbelievable!" I said. "I know him! He's so well respected and knows so much…"

"He would have a very good motive for trying to cover it up. He would lose prestige and credibility—I'm guessing his whole career would be gone. Isn't that what happened to the man you were talking about at the book club? The guy in England who forged a bunch of booklets?"

"Thomas J. Wise, yes. But he forged a lot of books."

"Weatherill might have done that, too. And he was evidently a lot more careful than Wise was."

I plodded on thoughtfully behind Molly. "It makes sense, I suppose. And Frank did send that email to him, telling him he thought he'd spotted a forgery. With Frank's store right next to the college, he probably guessed what forgery he was talking about."

Todd nodded. "And he decided Frank posed too much danger to be left alive."

"So are you going to arrest him?"

"We need to get some evidence. Right now it's all circumstantial. We might have enough to convict him of the original forgery, but even there we don't have any evidence that he ever came in contact with the water-stained book."

"You might. I got an email from Matt Wilkes, mostly

apologizing for his behavior. But he also mentioned that some expert, years ago, had taken three days to catalog and assess his great-grandfather's library. It was a point of pride for the old man, even though he apparently never read the books. I asked him if he could find out who that expert was. He hasn't responded yet, but I thought there might be a chance."

"Good. Very good, in fact. There's still nothing to tie him to any murders, but it's enough for us to justify keeping an eye on him and investigating him further."

"I suppose it's harder since he lives in Oregon. Different police departments and stuff."

"Exactly."

I grinned. "Well, I'm off school for the summer. I could tail him for you, if you like…"

This time it was Todd who stopped walking. "That's not even funny, Katrina." His voice was serious, reproving.

"Sorry," I said, abashed. "I was just kidding. I know I'd make a mess of it, with no training or anything."

"That's not what I meant."

I was completely lost.

"The thought of you out there, unprotected, trying to follow a killer around—" He broke off and ran his hand through his hair. "Sorry, that wasn't supposed to come out this way."

"What wasn't? What way?"

"I need to spell it out, do I?"

I think I nodded, but I'm not sure. I might have just stood there looking stupid. At any rate, he went on.

"I've been in love with you for weeks. You must have figured that out."

The shock of this announcement took my breath away. After a moment I recovered my wits enough to say, "Kim and Becky thought so, but I wasn't sure. You didn't say anything to me about it." Molly sat down, having apparently decided it was useless to pull on the leash anymore.

"I knew I couldn't talk to you about it until you knew I was divorced—full disclosure, and all that. And when I did tell you, I saw your face." He'd been looking at the ground, but he looked up then. "You looked horrified."

I started to feel a little sick. "I'm so sorry," I said. "I didn't know…"

He grabbed my hand. "No, don't feel that way. I didn't blame you. I just thought it was hopeless. I tried to stop caring, and I almost managed it until you popped up again when the manuscript was stolen."

"That's why you were so distant at first!"

"I tried to be. But you were just too adorable. I felt myself falling even more for you. But then you told me that you might go be a missionary." He gripped my hand more firmly. "Look, I don't want to get in the way if God wants you to go to teach at a mission school. And if you're interested in this guy Jason, I don't want to get in the way of that, either." He stopped and shook his head. "That's not quite honest. What I *want* is for you to stay here and be interested in me. But even if your life is going to go in another direction, at least you should know what I'm thinking. It was probably pretty obvious that I liked you— it must have been if your friends noticed—and I was beginning to be afraid you would think I was only flirting with you. I almost told you several times, and I should have. I just kept hoping that if we had more time to get to know each other, you'd be more likely to say yes."

He noticed just then that he was still gripping my hand, and he gently let it go.

"I knew there were tons of reasons you might not be interested in me. I'm divorced—I don't seem to be able to solve any crimes at all—there was another man who was asking you out—you might be called to be a missionary…When I thought about it like that, I couldn't believe you'd be willing to take a chance on me. But then when we were together, you were so friendly that I began to hope you might."

"God has been working on my heart," I said. "My prejudices against second attachments—" I almost made allusion to Marianne Dashwood discovering the falsehood of her own opinions here but stopped myself just in time. It was a good thing, too, because I wouldn't have had time to explain it. Almost as soon as I had stopped talking, we were aware of a Suburban speeding down the road. As it neared us, it slowed down, and I could see that Ed was driving it.

"Hey!" he said, and he looked panicked. "Have you seen Mia?"

"Not recently," I said. "When I came to your house first she was playing outside."

"No one's seen her since," said Ed. "It's not like her to run off."

"No, it's not," I agreed. Ben was the one who liked to run. Mia was extremely attached to her foster family. It was even hard for them to get her to go to school sometimes.

"Kim's afraid the birthmother may have done something. I don't think it's likely, but we still can't find her."

"Oh no!" I said. "Todd, Mia's birthmother made a big scene last week when they had a meeting, saying nothing could keep her from her daughter and that she was going to take her back. She's not stable at all!"

"I'll make a call," said Todd. "We'll start searching."

"Her mother just got out of prison," I said. "Would

223

she have a parole officer?"

"It depends," said Todd, "But if her daughter is in foster care, it shouldn't be too hard to find out where she lives. Same agency as the one we helped at the Fun Day for?"

"Yeah," said Ed. "You want to drive back to the house with me?"

"Good idea," said Todd. "You ok to walk back with the dog, Katrina?"

"Sure," I said. "I might just walk around nearby to see if I see her. It doesn't seem likely, but she may have wandered off or followed a stray cat or something."

"Ok," said Ed. Todd got into the car and they drove off.

I continued down the road with Molly, calling for Mia. I tried not to give way to alarm. Most kids have been "lost" at one time or another, only to be found shortly afterwards in some unexpected place. *Don't panic,* I kept telling myself. *Just pray.* I couldn't remember praying for anything so fervently in my entire life.

There were a few people out and about on the street—kids riding bikes, adults washing cars. I asked everyone I passed if they'd seen a little girl with dark hair come that way. No one had. Molly was beginning to slow down, and I found myself tugging on the leash to get her to walk faster.

I was just wondering if I should turn around and go back or try a different street when I saw the remains of a garage sale. It was early afternoon now, and they looked like they were deciding if they should start clearing up. I hurried over.

"Excuse me," I said to the couple who looked to be about my age. "Did you see a little girl go by—little girl with brown hair, about five years old? It might have been a while ago."

The wife frowned in thought. "You know, I think I did," she said. "It was about half an hour ago, maybe? I remember thinking she was too little to be out alone. She was running, and I thought maybe she was playing tag with someone, but no one else seemed to come after her."

"Which way did she go?"

The woman pointed farther down the street. "She might have been heading for the park. That's down that way."

"Of course!" I said. "Thanks!"

I started jogging in that direction, but then came to my senses and pulled out my phone.

"Todd?" I said when he answered. "I found a lady who saw a little girl about half an hour ago. She was headed in the direction of the park. I'm going to go there now, but I thought I should tell you."

"Great!" said Todd. "I'll meet you there."

I did run then and had every reason to regret not being in better shape. I arrived at the park's playground panting, sweating, and with a sharp pain in my side. I even felt slightly dizzy and was reminded that I had promised the doctor not to exercise for a couple months. There hadn't been the slightest chance I was going to exercise on purpose, but I couldn't have foreseen an emergency like this. There were lots of kids on the swings and slide, but none of them seemed to be Mia.

I was feeling more and more shaky, and when I saw the bench Kim and I had sat on a couple weeks ago I was able to get to it. I sat down, closed my eyes, and made myself concentrate on breathing. *In through the nose, out through the mouth. In through the nose, out through the mouth.* After a minute I felt better and opened my eyes. There were two kids standing in front of me staring at Molly. The big dog had flopped down at my feet, having probably never been led on such a forced march in her life. I couldn't imagine the trouble I would have getting her to walk home again.

"Can we pet your dog?" asked one of the boys. "Sure," I said. "Hey, have you seen a little girl with dark hair around here?"

The boys looked back at the playground and immediately I saw the absurdity of my question. There were a dozen little girls there, most with dark hair.

"Wait!" I said. There was a picture of Mia on my phone. I pulled it out and found it. "Here," I said. "Do you remember seeing this girl?"

One boy shook his head, but the other said, "I think so. She was over there." He pointed to a large bush.

"Thanks," I said, and suddenly remembered Mia crawling under a bush to hide. I looped Molly's leash around the arm of the bench and walked as quickly as I could manage over to the bush.

"Mia?" I called. I thought I heard movement inside the bush. I crouched down as best I could to peer between the branches. I saw a shoe. Mia's shoe. "Mia!" I said. "Are you ok?"

"Shhhhhh," came the reply. "Don't tell anyone I'm here."

Abandoning any dignity I might have had, I got onto my belly and crawled under the bush. It was part of a row of bushes, and there was actually space inside for me to sit up if I hunched over and avoided a big branch by leaning slightly to the right. Mia was lying down with her feet closest to me, but she sat up a bit when I got in there.

"Oh, Mia," I said, giving her as much of a hug as I could from my awkward position. "I was so worried about you! We couldn't find you!"

"I'm hiding," whispered Mia.

"From who?"

"From the policeman. He's going to take me back to my mom." Now that my eyes were adjusted to the shade, I could see streak marks of tears running down her face.

"No one's going to do that," I said.

"I heard her," Mia said. "I heard her say I was going to go back with her. And Mommy and Daddy got a new baby last night, and then today a police car came up and I knew he was going to bring me to my mom. There was a police car that came and got me when they brought me to Mommy and Daddy, so I knew that's what he was there for, to bring me back to my mom." Her face contorted. "I don't want to go!"

"Oh, Sweetie, Sweetie!" I said, hugging her tighter as she began to cry. "The policeman wasn't there for you. He just came to talk to me about something else." She continued to cry. "Listen, Mia. When your daddy couldn't find you, he told the policeman about it, and do you know what the policeman is doing right now? He's getting people together to help look for you to take you back to Mommy and Daddy. He knows your mom isn't allowed to have you right now, and he is making sure that she doesn't come and get you, ok?"

Mia nodded, but her emotions were still too strong to allow her to stop sobbing. I just held her and stroked her hair as best I could. When I thought she was a bit calmer, I said, "Hey, let's get out of here and go find your Mommy and Daddy, ok?"

She and I crawled out together and then we started walking back toward the bench where Molly still lay, mildly interested in the group of admiring children standing in a circle around her.

"Mia!" said Ed's voice behind us and we turned around to see him and Todd coming our way from the

227

parking lot.

"Daddy!" she screamed and ran toward him. He caught her up in his arms and hugged her for a long, long time.

Todd came up to me. "What happened?"

"She was hiding under a bush. She thought you had come to take her back to her birthmother. After the baby came last night she must have thought she was being replaced. And of course, her birthmother telling her she was coming to live with her again terrified her."

"Poor kid! Now I'm really sorry I didn't park the car elsewhere. Are *you* ok?"

"A little woozy," I said. I glanced down at my clothes and saw that they had been soiled by my contact with the ground. "And I'm dirty, too. I had to crawl under the bush to get to her. She wouldn't come out."

Todd smiled and reached up to my hair. At first I thought it was a tender gesture and I almost melted right there on the spot, but his hand came away again with a dried leaf that had been clinging to my hair.

"Oh!" I said.

"I'd better call off the search," said Todd. Ed was already calling Kim to tell her that he was with Mia, and Todd was soon on the phone with some other official person saying that the child had been found and reunited with her parents. I went back to Molly and sat on the bench while the men finished their calls. I was incredibly eager to continue my conversation with Todd. I replayed in my mind as much of his speech as I could remember, and probably had a silly smile on my face while I was doing it. I realized that I hadn't had much of a chance to say anything in return. In fact, I thought I'd only said something about God working on my heart before Ed had interrupted us.

I imagined us walking slowly back to the Coles' house together where I could tell him that I was deliriously happy to hear him say he wanted me to be with him, and that I had no intention of moving across the ocean or of dating Jason. It would be, after all, like the walk that Captain Wentworth and Anne took after he had opened his heart to her in that amazing letter.

I saw the men coming toward me and I stood up to meet them. Immediately I sat back down again. The adrenaline that had been keeping me going had evidently ebbed away after Mia had been found, and I felt much too weak to stand up, let alone walk back. I glanced at Molly and knew that she wasn't going to want to walk home, either.

"Let's go," said Ed. "We'll all go in the Suburban."

"Can you make it to the car?" asked Todd.

"I think so," I said.

"Well, take my arm," he said, and we walked like that across grass to the parking lot. It would have been much more romantic if I hadn't spent the whole time trying to stay upright instead of fainting, but I will say there have been very few strolls that I enjoyed more.

Ed and Kim insisted on my staying over that night. They said it was to keep an eye on me after all my exertions, but I knew it was mostly because Kim wanted to know what Todd and I had said to each other on our walk. When we'd gotten back to the house from the park, Tod had told us he needed to get back to the station. But while the Cole family were gathered around Mia, hugging her and each other, Todd had pulled me aside and asked if he could see me on Monday night.

"And you told him…?" said Kim later as we sat on Deirdre's bed like two teenagers discussing their first crushes. Deirdre had volunteered to give me her room while she slept on an air mattress in Mia's room.

"I said yes," I said. "He's picking me up at seven."

Kim squealed and hugged a pillow. "Where are you going? What are you doing? What are you going to *wear*?"

"No idea. About any of those things."

Kim twirled her hair as she thought. "Dressy casual. That will work for just about any activity."

I sat up straight suddenly. "Kim! I've just remembered! What will I do if Jason calls again?"

"He won't," she said calmly.

"How do you know?"

"I told him not to. A couple weeks ago. He asked if you were well enough to go out and I told him that something was developing with someone else—someone you already knew. I told him he should wait and see what happened with that relationship before trying again."

"Thanks. I hope that didn't hurt his feelings."

"I don't think so. I think he'd been testing a possibility but he hadn't made up his mind that you were the one for him or anything."

"Good."

"Now, you need to get to sleep." She picked up the empty mugs we'd drunk hot chocolate out of, along with the wrapper of the chocolate chip cookies we'd snuck into the room.

"I'll do my best," I said.

"Sweet dreams." Kim giggled like a fourth grader and I threw a pillow at her as she left the room.

CHAPTER 17

On Monday I spent way too much time picking out an outfit to wear that evening. It worried me a bit. I couldn't recall being flustered over a date to this extent since my early twenties. As the time approached, I made myself stop fiddling with my appearance. I looked at the clock. Six o'clock; I had an hour left. I thought I ought to read something to calm my nerves. I sat down on the sofa just as my phone dinged to tell me that I'd just gotten an email, so I read that first.

To: dr.kpeters@wilkester.edu
From: mjwilkes@wilkester.edu
Subject: re: Sorry

Dear Dr. Peters,

I asked a lot of people in my family if they knew the name of the man who had spent time looking at my great-grandfather's library. The only person who remembered him was my great-grandpa's old housekeeper. She wasn't positive, but she thought his name was Willoughby or something like that. At first she said it was Wuthering, but I think she was mixing it up with a novel. Anyway, that's all I could find out. I hope it helps.

Matt

Well, there was confirmation. I was glad my own little bit of detective work had paid off. I could hardly wait to tell Todd and see his reaction.

I reached over to the coffee table for my big, fancy edition of *Our Mutual Friend*. A student had once heard that it was my favorite of Dickens' novels and had given me this large-print leather-bound copy as a gift. It's somewhat impractical, as it's too much to carry around—at a thousand pages it looks more like a photo album—but it does look nice on a coffee table. I've read it so many times that I usually just skip to my favorite parts, so I read about John and Bella's long talk after Betty Higden's funeral, sympathising in a new way with their walk to the train station.

The doorbell rang just as John and Bella were getting onto the train, and I looked up at the clock. It was only six-thirty. Todd must be early, I thought. Either he'd gotten the time wrong or he just couldn't wait to see me. I stuck my finger in my place in the book and carried it with me to the front door. For a moment I entertained the idea of making some kind of joke about the book, like that I thought reading it aloud would make the perfect date, or that we couldn't leave until I had finished the whole thing. I hadn't decided which of these mild witticisms to use by the time I got to the door.

It didn't matter, because it wasn't Todd at the door. It was Dr. Weatherill.

I just stood there gazing at him unbelievingly. I had spent all weekend thinking he was somewhere in Oregon, and now he was standing in front of my door.

"Miss Peters?" He was perfectly polite and deferent,

just the same as I had seen him twenty-odd years ago, only more gray and thin than I remembered him.

"Yes?" I said, trying to appear calm.

"I wonder if I might have a word with you? You may not remember me, but you were in one of my classes at UCSC. Dr. Weatherill."

"Oh, right!" I said and pasted on a smile. "What is it you need?"

"Well, I'd like to come in and ask you a question—about your bookstore, as it happens. I don't know if you got a message I sent you by way of a third party."

"Yes, you said you might be interested in buying some of my books. I was very happy to hear that. Maybe we can arrange to meet sometime and go over the books together."

"I'd like to do that. But I still have a question. May I come in?"

If I've learned anything from mystery novels and TV shows, it's that you don't let murder suspects into your house when you're alone.

"Now isn't really a good time. I'm going to be leaving soon," I said. "Maybe you could come back tomorrow?"

He sighed. I noticed now that his eyes were bloodshot and he looked unwell.

"I'm afraid I must insist," he said and took his hand out of his coat pocket. It was holding a gun.

I froze, staring at it. He had killed Frank in daylight in his own store, and he would probably not hesitate to do the same to me. I wondered if I could keep him talking for half an hour, until Todd would show up.

I backed away from the door and let him enter. I still had *Our Mutual Friend* clutched to my chest. I'd remembered reading about a Bible carried in the shirt pocket of a soldier in World War I, was it? Or World War

II? Anyway, it stopped a bullet from killing him. I kept the book in front of me as a kind of shield. Just in case.

"I was wondering," Weatherill said, when he'd come in and shut the door, "where your safe is."

"I don't have a safe," I said.

"I mean the safe for the bookstore."

"But there isn't one," I said.

"Oh, yes there is. There's a secret safe." Weatherill's voice had taken on an edge.

"Really, I don't think there is." Frantic escape plans flitted through my head. Perhaps I could tell him I would show him the safe but he'd have to come with me, and then on the way I would signal someone or something. Or I could tell him that the police knew everything and he'd better give himself up instead of adding to his crimes. Surely he'd be to see the sense in that.

"I *know* there is," he said. "Frank Delaney told me in an email that there was a safe."

"He did?" I wondered if there'd been an email we never saw, because the one the police had found didn't mention anything about a safe. And Frank and I had had that discussion right before he died about the possibility of getting a safe. I didn't see how Frank could have had one.

"Well, he didn't tell me about it," I said.

"I think he did," said Weatherill. "I think he told you there was a book that needed to be kept secure. That's why it wasn't at his house or your apartment or the bookstore."

I would have been completely at sea if I hadn't already known what he was talking about. I decided to play very dumb.

"I don't understand," I said. I wondered if I could get to my phone, which was still lying on the sofa arm. I started moving slowly in that direction, walking backwards with the book still clutched in front of me.

"It's very simple," he said, speaking like I was five years old. "Frank Delaney had a secret safe, and he put a book I need into it."

"How do you know it was secret?" I said.

"He told me in code," said the professor. "He wrote, 'everything is safe for now.' You see? That was a message for me. It mentioned the word 'safe' but not in a way that most people would recognize it. It was a code language."

The idea of Frank making up any kind of code was completely laughable. *He's crazy*, I thought. That freaked me out more than anything else had done since I'd opened the door. There would be no reasoning with him if he was really out of his mind. All I could do would be to try to keep him calm. I looked at the clock on the wall. It was only six thirty-five; I wondered if I could keep him talking for twenty-five whole minutes. *Lord, help me*.

"Speaking of codes," I said, "I've always wondered about the code William Byrd used for his journal. Was it the same as Pepys?"

"No. Pepys used Shelton's system of shorthand, and Byrd used Mason's. But that doesn't answer my question about the safe."

I was almost to the sofa now but couldn't figure out how to pick up and use the phone without him knowing it.

"I really don't know anything about a safe," I said, "but it seems to me I read somewhere that Pepys used bits of other languages as well as shorthand in some of the more naughty diary entries. Is that true?"

"Of course it is." Weatherill's impatience seemed to be growing. "That's common knowledge. If you don't know that, then it's no wonder you're only an adjunct professor at a school like Wilkester!"

Amazing isn't it, that at such a moment my pride was still hurt by his statement?

235

"You're right," I said, swallowing the insult in the interest of safety. "But you know so much about all of literature. I'm sure *every* fact seems like common knowledge to you."

He appeared a little mollified. "Well, I have been immersed in the world of letters for a long time and have an extremely retentive memory." He moved closer to me but lowered the gun a bit.

"Did you know," I said, "When I was a freshman at UCSC I asked an English professor something about Guppy in *Bleak House*, and the professor said he'd never read it!" That was true, by the way. I'll never forget the shock it was to learn that an English professor had not read every novel written in English.

Weatherill snorted. "I'll bet that was Culbertson, wasn't it? He wasn't worth hiring. I told them so at the time. His specialization was free verse poetry. No scholarship needed at all to analyze that stuff! Anything goes, any interpretation is as valid as another. The thoughts of a ten-year-old about the poem are just as likely to be taken seriously as a scholar of forty years' standing. Authorial intent not an issue. Bah!" He was almost conversational now.

"It's not everyone that has the brain for true scholarship," I said. "You are unique."

Flattery, as E. L. Konigsburg said, is as important a machine as the lever: give it a proper place to rest and it can move the world. It moved the deranged mind of Dr. Weatherill.

"I am unusual, yes," he said. "The things I have undertaken—not one person in a million has the capacity to do the same."

"*Proper* interpretation of pre-twentieth century poetry, now that is what takes vast amounts of knowledge."

I leaned casually against the arm of the sofa. I couldn't yet reach my phone undetected, but I thought that if he got distracted somehow, I might have a moment to snatch it and use it. "It's not merely the language that most students have a hard time with, it's the classical allusions they don't get."

"Exactly!" He made the old gesture with his hands that I remembered from classroom days; it looked a little different with a gun in his hand. "I've been saying it for thirty years and no one will listen. Just like Milton and Shakespeare classes are required for every English major, a class on Aristotle and Virgil should be compulsory."

He was only about five feet away from me now, and I wondered if I could throw the book at him and make a run for it. I only considered it for a second; with my lack of athletic skill I'd probably miss him, or just barely touch him. Then I'd have to get to the door, open it, and run down the hallway to the staircase all the while hoping he couldn't hit me with a bullet. The odds of it working were not good.

"This is all very interesting," said Dr. Weatherill, "but we need to get back to the topic of the safe."

"But I don't know anything about a secret safe," I said. "I'd tell you if I did. You could take whatever you wanted out of it. But I still don't know anything about it."

He sighed. "That is really too bad. I can't just leave you here, you know. You've seen me with a gun."

"But you didn't do anything to me," I said. "It's not like you have anything to cover up."

He laughed. "Nothing to cover up! My dear lady, you have no idea. And I refuse to be brought to book merely because I left you alive to tell tales."

"Wilkester Police!" came a voice from outside, and the door was flung open at the same moment. Todd came in, gripping his gun with both hands, arms straight out in

237

front of him.

The relief I felt was tremendous. I expected an entire squad of policemen to come in behind him, but Todd remained the only officer there. "Put your gun down, Dr. Weatherill," he said.

For an older man, Weatherill moved quickly. With his free hand he grabbed my arm, which was still clutching Dickens, and pulled me out away from the sofa. He positioned himself behind me.

"Put *your* gun down," he said to Todd. "Or I'll be forced to shoot her."

"If you hurt her, it will be the last thing you do." Todd's voice was calm but carried conviction.

"Then we are at an impasse," said Dr. Weatherill, and I was irresistibly reminded of *The Princess Bride*.

"It's no good," I said. "We have no iocane powder for the battle of wits."

"What?" said Weatherill. At that moment I heard the wail of a siren.

"Oh, look," I said, turning toward the window beyond Weatherill as if I could see the street from it. "Here come the rest of the police cars."

Weatherill was distracted enough to try to see out the window, which meant he turned away from me. I gripped *Our Mutual Friend* with both hands and aimed for his head. I felt the book make contact with him and he staggered back. I dove down to the floor in case any shooting started and automatically closed my eyes.

No shots were fired, but there was a lot of thumping and grunting, and when I opened my eyes again, Weatherill was on the ground, face down, the gun was across the room, and Todd was kneeling beside him, pointing a gun at his back.

"Put your hands on the back of your head," said

Todd. "And stay still." Without moving his head or looking at me, Todd said, "Are you all right, Katrina?"

"Yes," I said.

"Nice shot with the book," he said. "That was a crazy thing to do and I hope you never, ever do anything like it again, but it did the job."

"Thanks. Are you going to put handcuffs on him?"

"I'll have to wait for backup to arrive," he said. "I'm off duty, and don't usually carry handcuffs with me. It will take them a few minutes to get here."

"But I heard them!"

"That was an ambulance, not a police car." He grinned. "Excellent distraction, though."

It really was only a few minutes before more police arrived. Dr. Weatherill was handcuffed and led out to a police car, his gun was bagged and taken away, and Todd and I drove in his car to the police station to make statements.

"This really wasn't the kind of date I was anticipating when I asked if you would see me tonight," Todd said as he drove down the road toward Wilkester.

I had to laugh. "Me neither. But it's a first date we'll never forget."

"I wouldn't have forgotten our first date, no matter what we did on it," said Todd. "But I agree that this was extra-memorable."

"How did you know he was in my apartment? And it wasn't even seven o'clock yet."

"I got there really early," he said. "I didn't want to be late for our date. I was just going to stay in my car until seven. Then I noticed a car parked out in front of your building with Oregon plates. We'd just started investigating Weatherill last weekend and his license plate number was fresh in my mind. It was his car. I barely paused to call for backup before I came charging up to your place." He stopped and swallowed. "I knew that he had shot Frank with no warning, and I was horribly afraid I was going to burst in and see he'd done the same thing to you. I had no idea how long he'd been there, you see."

"He just kept asking me about a secret safe that he claimed Frank had. He said in that email Frank sent him, 'everything is safe' meant 'everything is *in* a safe" in some kind of code language. I think he's gone a bit crazy."

"Yes, he looked—and acted—not quite sane. Impossible to say, for sure. Guilt can do a lot of things to a person. His thinking certainly has gotten twisted."

It took a long time for Todd to write out his report and for me to be interviewed as a witness. By the time we were finished it was nearly nine thirty and we were beyond starved.

"Sally's is open," Todd said.

We sat in the same booth we'd sat in after the book club. This time we ordered chicken pot pie and hot biscuits. It tasted divine.

"You know, I think this is the finest restaurant in the city," I said.

"I think you were very hungry," said Todd, "but it *is* good."

"Maybe it's the company that makes it so enjoyable to eat here," I said.

"Maybe." He smiled and my heart fluttered. This time I didn't smack it down.

"Listen, Katrina," he said, pushing his nearly-empty plate aside and leaning toward me, resting his forearms on the table in front of him. "I told you what I was thinking and feeling last Saturday, and then we were interrupted before you could tell me what you thought of it. All you were able to say was that God had been working on your heart regarding second attachments, and I've been clinging to hope all weekend on the strength of that. That, and the fact that you agreed to see me tonight. You don't seem like the kind of woman who accepts a date only to tell the guy she wants to remain friends."

I had to laugh. "No, I'm not."

"So tell me, please. Is a relationship with me a possibility?" *'The expression of his eyes overpowered her'*… *So this is what Mr. Knightley looked like when he proposed to Emma!* I pulled myself together enough to say something coherent.

"Yes," I said. "It is."

He grinned. "What about you going overseas?"

"I'd already decided not to teach at the mission school."

"And what about Jason?"

"You got here first," I said. "Kim already told Jason to hold off asking me again."

"Bless her," said Todd fervently.

I shook my head. "I feel like our relationship has been stage-managed. Between her telling Jason not to ask me and Ed arranging for you and me to work together at that Family Fun Day…"

"What? That wasn't Ed. That was me."

"That was you? You planned that?"

He nodded. "I asked John—Detective Ortega—if he could arrange that I be paired up with you. He's good friends with the lady that was organizing it, so they made it happen."

"Oh!"

"I was hoping for a chance to explain about the divorce. And to spend time with you in some setting that didn't involve detective work."

"Well," I said, "I'm probably one of the few people on the planet for whom an interrogation room can hold pleasant memories."

Todd raised his eyebrows.

"The first moment of comfort I had after the shooting," I went on, "was when you looked me in the eyes and told me I was handling it well."

"You were," he said. "But you had me at the very beginning when you didn't want to be called Ms."

"I remember that. As soon as I said it I was afraid you would think I wanted to make sure you knew I was single, because I was after you or something. But of course I didn't realize how it would sound until after I said it. I was really embarrassed."

"Just like when you told me I should spend more time with you if I wanted to see you say something silly? You are adorable when you blush. You're doing it right now."

"I know," I said. "I can feel my face getting hot."

"Shall I drive you home? Are you ok going back there?"

"I'm fine. I didn't think I would be, but I am."

Todd paid the bill and we walked out across the parking lot. Just like the last time, the air was mild, the moon was full, and we walked close together. This time we held hands.

Case Closed

All is well in Wikester again… for now.

Todd and Katrina have time to spend getting to know each other without the hassle of murder and mayhem.

Or do they?

You might think that a professor could expect at least a few weeks with her new boyfriend… errm… suitor! Um… beloved? But there is that pesky event coming up. Still, it shouldn't take up too much of Katrina's attention, right?

Austen, tea parties, and snuff boxes—the things of days past. Simple. Elegant. Deadly?

Buy *Snuffed Out* today (or keep reading for a sneak peek!).

Here's a sneak peek at book two in the Wilkester Mystery series:

SNUFFED OUT

Chapter 1

Wilkester College is generally quiet during the summer months. Just after school lets out in May they offer a few accelerated courses for two weeks—a semester's worth of class squashed into a fortnight. These courses are popular with those students who prefer intensive misery over a more extended tedium. During the rest of summer, the campus hosts various conferences and conventions, ranging from kids' sports camps to political think-tanks, and walking across the campus in July you might overhear conversations about thirteenth century Chinese art or the overall ineffectiveness of the primal scream psychotherapy technique.

I love the academic chatter on such a wide variety of topics. You can imagine yourself at Oxford or Cambridge for a moment…if you shut your eyes to the buildings around you. The style of architecture was considered modern in 1955, which means that the campus is made up mostly of unadorned concrete structures: giant off-white blocks with orangey-pink streaks caused by the incessant rain of Washington State spilling off the roofs with no overhang.

The one big exception in this cubists' paradise is the large lecture hall in the Johnson building. Whoever designed that knew what a college lecture hall should look like. It's a large room—seats five hundred—and has dark oak panels on the lower half of the walls. The windows above them are tall and have matching shutters, and the front wall of the room is entirely panelled in oak with medallions carved into the top row of panels. You really can imagine yourself at a European university in there.

"It's the perfect location for the Regency Conference general sessions," said Susan as we stood at the back of the hall and looked down toward the front—literally down, as each row of seats goes down a level to give everyone in the audience a fair view of the speaker.

"I agree," I said. "I only wish there were more lecture halls like this for the breakout sessions."

"Or something besides the gymnasium for the dancing lessons and the ball," said Susan. The Regency Conference was her brainchild. A professor of history, Dr Susan Langton was a dedicated scholar, an enthusiastic teacher and a masterful organizer. She was a small, thin woman in her mid-forties, and she wore her slightly-gray hair in a pageboy style that was always falling into her eyes. She had the habit of swooping her hair back out of her face with one hand at least once a minute. She did it again now, and I wondered for the hundredth time why she did not get some kind of clip for it, or even a different hairstyle.

This was the first year the college had put together anything like this conference. Usually, established groups rent the premises for their meetings, but this one had really sprung from the college itself. Several of the faculty were giving lectures and the catering would be provided by the college kitchen. A few experts were being brought in from outside to give instruction in English country dancing, period clothing, and late Georgian food, and the lecture offerings included topics on the history, literature, music, and society of the Regency period. More than two hundred attendees had registered, most of them from Seattle or Tacoma but a few from other states. About half of them were historical novelists hoping to make their fiction more authentic and accurate, and the others were history or literature students or teachers.

"Which lectures are you giving again?" asked Susan.

"One called 'Beyond Austen' about Regency authors other than Jane Austen, and 'From Novel to Movie' which is all about the strategies used in adapting a book to film."

"Ooo, I might sit in on those." She swooped her hair back again and sighed. "I hope everything will be ready by tomorrow. There's still so much to do."

"You'll get it done. I have every confidence in you."

"Oh, my part is pretty much completed, it's just coordinating everyone else. The printers can't deliver the campus maps until four o'clock, for one thing. And I thought the food was all set, too, but I got a note today to meet with someone tonight about a possible change to the menu to make it more authentic. I said it didn't matter but he was insistent." Her brow clouded in an uncharacteristically anxious expression. She seemed to be dreading the meeting.

"Can't you get out of it?" I said. "Send someone else?"

"No, I can do it. I'll be on campus anyway getting the nametags sorted and the welcome packets collated after the maps arrive."

"Do you need help?"

"No, I'll be fine. I'll recruit the history department

secretary to help me if I need more hands. Look, I'd better go. I'll see you tomorrow, ok?"

"Bright and early," I affirmed.

I'm not really at my best early in the morning, and by early I mean eight o'clock. Thankfully the session I was leading wasn't until after lunch, so my brain had time to wake up before I was called upon to be intelligible. I attended the morning general session, the topic of which was "The Importance of the Regency Period in the Shaping of the Modern World." It was a good lecture by someone I'd never heard of before, and I enjoyed myself. I've always been grateful that if I couldn't have my first choice of profession (that of housewife), I could at least have my second choice, which was to be a college professor. Even though the tenure track hadn't worked out and I had to pad my adjunct professor income with editing work, I still enjoyed what I did. I would have risen from my bed weeping every morning if I'd had any job that required a calculator or a spreadsheet.

I was looking forward to lunch by the time twelve-thirty came, and I was discomposed along with everyone else when we got near the cafeteria only to be told that there would be a half-hour delay in the serving of the mid-day meal. I caught sight of Susan from a distance hurrying along the main path through campus with someone who looked like a secretary at her heels. Even at twenty yards I could feel the nervous energy emanating from her and I wondered if it had to do with a crisis in the catering.

I suddenly remembered I'd left my briefcase with my lecture notes back at the Johnson building. It would probably be safe enough there, but with the delay in lunch I might as well get it now. There were a few people still in the lecture hall when I came in, the inevitable flotsam that washes up on the shores of post-lecture auditoriums. Two of them were middle-aged women who looked like authors, still chatting in their seats. From what I could hear it seemed that they were trying to impress each other with their average daily word counts and Twitter follower statistics. One man sat writing furiously on a notepad; he was either an author suddenly seized with inspiration or a college lecturer who was trying to reproduce the talk he'd just heard for the benefit of next semester's students. Someone else who looked administrative and vaguely familiar was digging through the trash can—probably he'd dropped his keys or something in there accidentally. I felt a surge of compassion for him: I've done the same thing a few times. Hopefully whatever he'd inadvertently tossed wasn't the keys to one of the classrooms we were using.

I grabbed my briefcase and headed back toward the dining hall. A line had formed and I joined it obediently, pulling out my lecture notes to review while I waited. I was pondering whether or not my little joke about antimacassars having nothing to do with being anti-massacre was worth keeping when I heard my name called by a masculine voice. I looked up to see Todd coming toward me. I wondered if the fluttery feeling that came whenever I saw him would go away after a while. It had been two months since we'd become a couple, and so far the flutters hadn't diminished at all.

"Hi!" I said as he came up to me. "What are you doing here?"

"I was in the neighborhood for lunch and thought I'd see if you were around. Have you given your talk yet?"

"No, it's right after lunch."

"Well, I hope it goes well. What time are you going to be finished with everything today?"

"The last session ends at four. I'm free after that."

"You want to go up to the forest then? I'm off duty

at three. I'll bring a picnic dinner and we can eat it on our rock. Weather like this is too good to waste."

"That sounds great! I'll meet you at my place at about four-thirty, ok?"

"Perfect!" The smile that had charmed me from the beginning appeared again, and with a cheery, "See you then!" he walked back the way he had come.

"Is that your boyfriend?" said the lady who was standing next to me in line and had evidently heard everything.

"No," I said. "I mean, yes." *Boyfriend* didn't seem the right word for Todd and I never thought of him as my boyfriend. For me the term conjures up the image of teenagers and I always think there should be another label for those over forty. *Suitor* would be my choice, but I doubt I could get the modern world to go along with it. *Lover* has changed meanings in the past hundred years and *beau* only sounds right if you have a Southern accent.

The lady looked at me as if I were completely air-headed. How could I not know if I was dating someone or not?

"We haven't been dating long," I offered feebly.

"Oh!" she said. "Well, if I were you, I'd hang on to that one pretty tightly. He's quite a catch!"

"He is, indeed." I wondered how often he had to fend off the advances of women who would have liked to catch him for themselves.

The line started moving then, and we eventually got our meal of white soup, beef cutlets, peas, potatoes and peach sorbet. The food was authentic enough, but it rather spoils the effect to eat it at a modern cafeteria table with your plate sitting on an orange plastic tray.

My talk went well if I do say so myself. My audience was mostly made up of literary scholars, but there was a handful of writers, most of whom had vague ideas about writing spinoffs of Maria Edgeworth's novels or Ann Radcliffe's or even Fanny Burney's. I mentioned during my lecture that my other professional hat was that of editor, so several of the writers came up afterwards and wanted to talk to me about book ideas.

When that was finished I wandered over to the gymnasium to watch the English Country Dancing lesson. For a minute I wished I could attend the ball the next evening. I watched the dancers prancing in time to the music and wondered if Todd liked to dance and if he'd be willing to try English country dancing. I was doubtful: there's rather a lot of skipping involved which most men find undignified. It was probably better not to ask at this point in the relationship. What if he felt pressured to try it and then didn't like it? I didn't want him stuck in an activity he didn't enjoy.

I sighed. So much of dating seems to be wondering— wondering what the other person likes and dislikes, wondering what you're doing or not doing that might be bothering them, wondering how deeply you ought to let yourself care for the person when they might end the relationship…

"I hate dating," I said aloud under the cover of "The Redesdale Hornpipe" blaring from the giant speakers set up on the bleachers.

Nonetheless I was looking forward to my evening out with Todd, and I wasn't disappointed. July is a great time to be in the Mr. Rainier National Forest. The drive up the mountain and the hike through the trees were idyllic. We had our own path to what we called "our rock"—a giant boulder that sits on the side of the mountain a little off the main trail. From its top you can see across a valley.

Todd had packed an insulated picnic bag with store-bought hoagie sandwiches, a bag of potato chips, and two bottles of water, and we sat on top of our rock and ate. The bag had an attractive blue and green chevron pattern and all kinds of pockets inside for the different items you might need if you had a very elaborate picnic.

"That's a nifty bag," I said. "Useful and attractive all in one."

"Yeah, it comes in handy."

I opened my mouth to ask where he'd bought it, but I was arrested by the thought that it might have been something left behind by his ex-wife. If it was, I'd rather not know.

"Oh!" I said suddenly. "I meant to tell you. Becky says she will probably get her first foster child in a couple days."

"Really? That seems awfully quick. I thought she just started the process a couple months ago."

"She was fast-tracked because she already had a lot of police clearances and training done for her job as a teacher. She thinks she's going to have a little girl placed with her—she doesn't know how old."

"She's probably pretty excited, huh?"

"Yeah, and nervous, too. 'Half agony, half hope'—but not for the same reason, of course."

Todd looked at me with a raised eyebrow.

"*Persuasion*," I murmured and cleared my throat. "What time is it?"

"Getting near seven."

"I know there's still a couple hours left before sunset, but I probably should be getting back home," I said. "I want to look over my notes for tomorrow's lecture."

We gathered what little trash we had and put it back in the bag. Todd went first down the rock and then turned to help me jump down the last few feet.

251

We'd only gone a couple yards back toward the car when I heard Todd say, "Hey, what's this?"

He picked up something off the ground and held it so I could see it. It was a little silver box with filigree on the sides and inlayed ivory in a flower pattern on the top.

"It looks like a mini-jewelry box," he said, "or maybe something for holding pills."

"No, it's a snuff box," I said. "What in the world would it be doing here? It's not like people carry them around anymore."

"So it's an antique?"

"That's the only kind there is. The only person I know of who has any is Susan—Dr Langton. She has a collection of about five in her office. She uses them for holding paper clips and thumbtacks and things."

"You don't suppose she dropped one here, do you?"

I laughed. "She's a little scatter-brained—the absent-minded professor, you know—but definitely not to the extent that she would be strewing snuff boxes on mountainsides."

"I think we ought to take this with us," said Todd. "If it's valuable, the owner might have alerted the police that it was lost or stolen."

"Sounds like a good idea."

"I wonder…" said Todd. He had begun walking but stopped again.

"What?"

"Well, if this was dropped, other things might have been dropped, too. It wouldn't be a bad place to dump something, actually."

"You mean like stolen goods?" I asked.

"Yeah. This is the kind of place where someone might temporarily stash something. It's off the regular trail and most people wouldn't go to the back side of the big rock—they'd perch on top of it, like we did. Putting something around the other side would be a good way to hide it."

We walked down the hill alongside the base of the big rock with Todd scanning the ground for any other items. When the hill got steeper he went on alone and I looked around the rocks and shrubs where I was.

"There's nothing that I can see down here," Todd called after a few minutes.

"I don't see anything, either," I said. "A few old empty cans and bottles—someone should really clean this up. There's an old shoe." I looked again. "Hey Todd, it looks like there's a bundle of something here. It's near a bush but there's rocks kind of piled around it, too."

Todd hurried up to where I was.

"See?" I said pointing. "There's the bottom of a shoe. With the way it's positioned I thought for a minute that it was a person lying there."

Todd went over to the bundle and bent over it.

"What is it? A stash of something?" I said coming over to him.

"Stay back, Katrina," Todd said in a different voice, holding up a hand.

"What is it?" I said again.

"It's a body."

If you enjoyed this excerpt, purchase *Snuffed Out* today! .

253

BOOKS BY BARBARA CORNTHWAITE

The Wilkester Mysteries
Brought to Book (Book 1)
Snuffed Out (Book 2)
Book 3

George Knightley Esquire:
Charity Envieth Not
Lend Me Leave

A Very Austen:
Christmas
Valentine
Romance

A Fine Young Lady

Printed in Great Britain
by Amazon